THE MANEATER

Mouse forced his own eyes to travel past the nervous colt and to move along the shadowed trail beyond the place where Patch Eye had buried the trap. The boy knew sheer terror then. Mato had come down to the bait. He was standing up there in the dark watching Mouse.

Mouse could just make him out, a gigantic black shadow against the twilight gloom of the mountain behind him. His head swung to and fro, searching the evening breeze. The boy heard him grunt softly, and knew he had scented the colt. Turning his gaze from him a moment to see how Heyoka was reacting, he looked back to find the trail empty. Mato had disappeared.

Mouse blinked hard. Could it have been his imagination playing tricks upon him? But no, shadows did not grunt and blow out softly through their nostrils. The boy shook with fear. Rolling his head as far as his bonds would permit, he scanned the edges of the meadow. Nothing there. Wait. What was that? Over there beyond Heyoka. In the blackness of the pines. Just where the trail came down from the mountain. It was Mato!

★★★★★★★★★★★★★★★★★★★★★★★★★

THE LEGEND
OF THE
MOUNTAIN

★★★★★★★★★★★★★★★★★★★★★★★★★

Will Henry

LEISURE BOOKS NEW YORK CITY

A LEISURE BOOK®

June 2003

Published by special arrangement with Golden West Literary Agency.

Dorchester Publishing Co., Inc.
276 Fifth Avenue
New York, NY 10001

Visit us on the web at www.dorchesterpub.com.

Table of Contents

The Friendship of Red Fox

The Sioux young men were nervous. The cavalry troops from three Army posts were pressing them very closely. Two times before their escape from Pine Ridge, other small bands of desperate Oglalas had tried to do the same thing—get away from the reservation and reach the remaining wild Sioux of Sitting Bull in Canada. Those other bands had been caught by the cavalry and brought back. The young men of the third band had sworn they would not go back—not alive. They could not endure the shame of Pine Ridge. They could not bear to have their old wild freedom changed, taken from them, destroyed.

If the cavalry should catch them, they would be glad to die in the business of war and take some of the Pony Soldiers to the Land of the Shadows with them. But more than dying, they wished to be free, to stay free, and to reach their people who had found freedom in the north. So it was that the Sioux young men grew nervous and began to think of ways in which the pursuing troops might be slowed down, discouraged, stopped, short of fighting them on purpose and to no avail save death for all.

"There is only one way, my brothers," said their leader, High Bear.

Of his six companions, five nodded their dark heads and said: "Yes, you are right . . . we must do it now."

The seventh Sioux said nothing. He was a boy only. Perhaps he had ten summers. His name was Tokeya Luta, Red Fox, and he had come unbidden with High Bear, who was his uncle, and the other young men. He had trailed them away from Pine Ridge, revealing himself only on the second day, when they could not send him back because of the cavalry. So he said nothing when the young men talked, fearing they might yet cut him off from their company, might yet vent upon him their rightful anger at his trick in coming after them.

The boy's heart grew small, however, when he heard the words of his companions. He knew what they meant when they said there was but one way in which they might now delay the Pony Soldiers. It was a very bad way, and Red Fox was unhappy to hear it spoken of, and to see the frightening looks with which the young men nodded to one another and turned their horses swiftly toward the low ridge to their right—the ridge they had intended using for cover to sneak past the lonely settlement farm and continue on their way to Wyoming.

So it was that High Bear's young men, pressed too hard by the closing troops from Nebraska, South Dakota, and their own Wyoming, desperate alike for fresh horses and for food for themselves and for a little time to rest, commenced killing. From that second day they vowed the narrowing line of their northwestward flight would be marked by dark and by day for the pursuing soldiers with signs no cavalryman could mistake. By day the troops would have to follow the circling swing of the buzzards, high in the sky, or the towering columns of greasy black smoke from the burning buildings. By night it would be even easier. High plains skies are blacker than the pit when there is no moon. Even a white Pony Soldier could see the red blaze of a wagon, barn, or cabin burning when the sun was down and only the stars hung out to wink and glitter against the overpowering darkness.

* * * * *

The sod-house woman put the last of the threadbare work shirts on the clothesline and turned wearily for the back stoop of the shanty and another armload of the week's wash. She was a tall woman, fadingly blonde, and might once have been attractive. But she walked now with the shambling gracelessness of the drudge who was no longer at war with the endless hard days that pulled at her thin shoulders, tortured her back muscles, drew the very life from her skin.

The utterly desolate outlands of northwestern Nebraska did these things to the wife of a twenty-cow homesteader, a sodbuster who had neither the brains nor the sensitivity to realize that God and nature wanted him here no more than did the Sioux, the Arapahoes, and the Cheyennes. As the woman moved, head down and listless, a rider came into distant view over the prairie. She looked up, shoulders straightening. A hint of happiness stirred her lips, spread to her tired eyes.

The 3rd cavalry's regular mail rider between Fort Farewell, Nebraska, and Fort Fetterman, Wyoming, was a day early, she thought. This may have seemed small enough reason for the trace of joy that made the woman's face younger for the little time it lingered there. Yet such was the desolation of Amy Lohburg's life that this rider's dependable 'appearance was its sustaining faith.

Dutch Lohburg, her husband, was a man who said little and understood less of the human feelings beyond hunger, labor, desire. To *talk* of anything was alien to his nature; *doing* was Dutch Lohburg's forte. The soldiers, on the other hand, were younger men and, like Amy, not out in this empty land by choice. They, too, yearned for home—wherever that was, or whatever it meant—and wanted, as did the lonely sod-house woman, to speak of the hope of seeing it again. Just the hope, really. None of them expected to get home soon, if ever, and only prayed, as Amy Lohburg prayed, for a transfer from this hell to some lesser one where each new day was not a blasphemy or blight upon the human spirit.

So the prairie woman hastened to smooth her soiled dress and to push back the work-moistened tangle of her hair. She must go put on the coffee pot and set a pan of rolls to rise. As well, one of the four children must be rounded up and sent to find Dutch, who, while taciturn, was hardly inhuman and appreciated in his inarticulate way the chance to see and be with another man. As near as he ever came to smiling, that near Dutch Lohburg came when the Army mail rider stopped for coffee and to water his horse at the Lohburg place.

In her flustered pleasure at the soldier's day-early arrival, Amy did not at first note anything unusual about the manner of his approach. Then she did. Too long on the prairie to miss an alien fact for more than a moment, she stopped and did not go into the house. The soldier wasn't loping his horse, or trotting him; he was running him full out. Indeed, even as she hesitated fearfully, he was within hail and had waved and shouted to her. Next moment, he slid his lathered mount up to her and dismounted.

" 'Morning, ma'am. Didn't aim to alarm you dashing up this way. Hope you didn't drop any wet wash."

The rider was not one of the regular mail carriers. He was a homely giant of a first sergeant, with a wide-toothed grin and a quiet, steady way about him that put a skip not born of fear in the heart of Amy Lohburg. An exchange of eye searching followed, and, when it was over, Sergeant Frank Fenton had also felt the tongueless language of the lonely and the longing.

"Soldier," said the woman, "what's the matter? You rode in here as if you'd seen a ghost . . . or been chased by one."

"Not one, ma'am . . . seven."

Her gray eyes narrowed. "Indians?"

"Yes, ma'am."

"Well, dust yourself off and come in. Water basin's on the stoop. I'll put the coffee on."

Being chased by Indians was not news in northwest Nebraska—not ordinarily. But the big sergeant moved quickly to cut her off from the shanty kitchen.

"Missus Lohburg, ma'am, there's no time for coffee. Where's your kids?"

"Oh, God," said Amy Lohburg quietly. "Bad Indians?"

Fenton nodded. "As bad as any ever were. They're Sioux, broke out from Pine Ridge and heading for Canada to join up with Sitting Bull. Cavalry's been after them forty-eight hours, and they've turnt desperate. Started to . . . well, you know."

She nodded in return, saying nothing.

Weeks ago the commanding officer at Fort Farewell had urged the few whites in his forgotten corner of Nebraska to come in and stay on the post until the rash of Sioux outbreaks at the reservations could be quelled. But, like too many unfearing frontiersmen before him, Dutch Lohburg had refused to "stompede." He was of the wrong-headed kind who, because they could not understand the horseback Indians, could not be afraid of them. Oh, be careful of them, keep a watch out for the red devils, but as far as being run out by them, nonsense! They could be handled by any white man of experience who owned a proper share of courage and a modern repeating rifle. Dutch Lohburg had both.

"Ma'am," said the sergeant, ending the five-second silence, "I asked you where your kids was. Come on, now. Get yourself together."

His repeated insistence about the children, with no word of her husband—the first thing a Western man would ask about in an Indian situation—brought a sudden shadow of premonition to the tall woman.

"Why don't you ask me where my husband is, Sergeant?"

"I know where your husband is, Missus Lohburg."

"Oh, no."

"He never had a chance, ma'am. They shot him to pieces. They was after the cattle. I found three fresh hides from skinned-out beeves just beyond where I found your husband."

"The spring heifers," said the woman dully. "Dutch got the bull and the cows into the home corral yesterday . . . you can see them yonder . . . but the heifers hid out on him. He and Billy started out this morning early to. . . ." She broke off, voice rising. "The boy was with Dutch! I'd forgotten he was with him! Oh, dear God."

The sergeant seized her roughly and shook her until she stopped moaning.

"Listen, now," he said. "I think your boy is all right, you hear me? I didn't find him with your husband, and I think I saw him with the Sioux."

"You saw the Sioux?"

"They jumped me when I rode up on them skinning out those beeves. I was following the buzzards. I was sent out here, special, to bring you all into Farewell. So I figured it was trouble when I seen them vultures circling overhead."

"And Billy? You think the Sioux have him?"

"Certain of it." Fenton wasn't certain of it, but he had to make the woman believe he was. Besides, he did *think* he had seen an eighth horseman, not an Indian, in the instant before he legged back up on his cavalry mount and ran for his life away from that place where the buzzards were gathering. "You see, ma'am, them horse Indians is crazy about boy kids, even white ones. I figure they grabbed your Billy and mean to take him with them."

Amy Lohburg accepted it, understanding she had no choice but to do so. "I'll get the girls. They've been playing out yonder in the harness shed. We'll take the bay team, I think, and the spring-bed wagon. Will you go with us, Sergeant?"

"I can't, ma'am. There's the Haraldsens up on Spring Creek. Not likely they're in the line of march of this bunch, but my orders include them. I'd feel bounden to go up anyways."

"Yes, of course. I think they're already gone, though."

"But you ain't sure?"

"No. They didn't come by here."

They both knew that decided it. It was the type of option all too often granted on the frontier. There were simply never enough soldiers to go around, and always too many Indians.

"I'll hook up the team, Missus Lohburg. Take a few things with you . . . blankets and such. But hurry it up."

"How much time do we have?" It was not a wasting question, did not indicate uncertainty or hesitation.

"Our troops are right on them, maybe half a day back, no more. But them Indians got to rest, too. They been moving over two days straight, and fast. Their horses won't take it without a lay-over. I reckon, with the beef to cut up and pack for carrying, figuring time to cook and eat and sleep, they'll spend five hours back there, four anyways. Then it's only a short hour's ride up to here. Call it six hours, ma'am."

"And you think they will come here?"

"They've got to, Missus Lohburg. They're after cattle, guns, ammunition, any supplies you people may have. Also, they're after *you*. Every time the cavalry has to stop and bury somebody or . . . well, you understand. They'll be here, ma'am, certain as sunrise. Gather up your things and your kids. And if you're a good pray-er, start praying."

It was neither an ignorant nor an accidental note upon which he concluded, but rather the necessary knife twist of reality. Amy Lohburg, grimacing to the thrust, went swiftly toward the stock corral and the three little tow-headed girls playing in their dead father's harness shed twenty-eight miles northwest of Fort Farewell, Nebraska, and, all unknowingly, less than twenty-eight *minutes* northwest of High Bear and his escaped pack of Pine Ridge Sioux.

Beyond the stock corral, out past the winter hayrick on the Lohburg place, a deep dry wash ran southward into the drainage of the Red Butte meadows. Up out of the cover of this wash, while the dust of the Army sergeant's horse was still dying away toward the Haraldsen homestead, came High Bear and three Oglala shadows. There was a fourth shadow, but it was not Oglala. Feet bound together under the belly of his rough-coated pony, mouth gagged so that he might not cry out, Billy Lohburg was a very pale shadow, indeed.

The Sioux sat their mounts noiselessly as the noon wind. They watched the white woman down in the ranch yard. She was putting the last of three small girl children into a rickety wagon behind a team of bays. The Indians waited while the woman carefully hid the children, making them lie down in the wagon bed, covering them with old feed sacks and household bedding, talking to them, calming them, yet working with knowing speed.

"*He-hau,*" grunted one of the two braves with High Bear. "The woman is a good mother. See how she hides the little ones."

"A true thing, Crow Killer," agreed Big Nose, the second man. "See how quick yet careful she is. She is not afraid."

"She is the wife of the hard dier back there where we found the young cattle," said High Bear. "He was not afraid, either."

The third follower, the third of the Oglala shadows, was not a man, and he said nothing. Red Fox had been brought along only to lead the pony on which Billy Lohburg rode, a great enough honor, indeed, but not entitling him to be heard in a company of warriors.

"Well,"—Crow Killer shrugged, looking at his friend, Big Nose—"how will it go with this woman? With her and the three girls there? Yes, and with this yellow-haired boy we have with us?"

"A good question," approved Big Nose. "I think we better not let any of them get away. Maybe we better even kill this yellow-haired boy."

"Yes." Crow Killer nodded quickly to the suggestion. "He cannot ride well enough to keep up with us."

They were looking at Billy Lohburg.

Billy understood he was being discussed—and not in a friendly way. He understood, as well, that his mother and sisters were in deadly peril, although the Sioux were not scowling or ugly about it but only talking it over, as though to decide whether to pay a call or go on.

The white boy looked desperately at the Oglala youth who sat the pony next to his, holding the lead rope to his own mount.

Red Fox felt his companion's fears. He kneed his pony closer to that of the white boy. Billy and he had exchanged no word since the white boy's capture. The latter believed this to be because the Indian boy spoke no English, for he had not replied to Billy's attempts to talk with him. The reason, however, was that Red Fox was also afraid. His adult companions were in a great deal of trouble. They would be in more trouble now that the Pony Soldier rider—the huge three-stripe soldier—had gotten away from High Bear and the others and would reach Fort Fetterman with the latest story of the Sioux position. The big sergeant might even find a cavalry troop before he got to the fort, and then the Sioux would have to fight. This meant dying. Red Fox, the same as his older companions, did not want to die; he wanted to find Sitting Bull upon the land of the Red River mixed-blood Indians of Canada. He wanted to live and to be free again.

He put his dark hand out and squeezed the hand of his white prisoner. At the same time he shook his head sharply and put a finger to his lips, motioning with his head toward High Bear and the others.

Billy Lohburg was a bright lad, and brave enough. He bit his lip and nodded back to Red Fox. He understood.

"Let me see." High Bear had said little, as he sat studying the Lohburg place and the hurried activity of Amy Lohburg. Now he spoke with real care. "The woman is strong. No doubt she can get to Fort Farewell in only a few hours. Then the soldiers will know exactly where we are."

"Yes, yes." Crow Killer was showing the first excitement. "Then that Pony Soldier who got away from us, he will be at Fort Fetterman saying the same thing in only a little while longer. We will be in the jaws of a trap. I say kill all these people and go after that soldier fast. We can catch him."

"No," said High Bear. "His horse is better than ours. Let him go. Besides, he fought well. He knocked you two great fighters off your ponies. I should think you would want to forget him."

"Never!" vowed Crow Killer. "But we can come back for him another time. Right now, the thing to do is get rid of that woman and the little girls."

"Yes." Big Nose was growling a little now. "And this nuisance of a blue-eyed boy, here. He's no good. Why did you want to keep him in the first place? Eh? Answer that."

High Bear shrugged. He was a tall Indian, and handsome.

A nephew of the great American Horse, the Oglalas' finest fighter next only to Crazy Horse, he knew no fear of such complainers as Big Nose and Crow Killer. Yet they were dangerous men, and desperate. He answered very carefully.

"I saved the white boy to take to Sitting Bull. I am told that the old chief grows lonely. He raised a white boy once, you know. He loved him very much. But that boy is gone, and I thought the old man would be happy with another one to take his place." He stared at his two sullen comrades. "What are you taking to Sitting Bull to show your gratitude?"

"High Bear may have something," said Crow Killer. "I brought nothing. I had no time. We left too fast."

Big Nose, a practical Indian, shrugged. "I will worry about a gratitude present when I see Sitting Bull," he said. "Right now, I feel very far away from him."

"True." High Bear nodded. "What do you say about the white boy?"

"Kill him," said Big Nose.

"Quickly," amplified Crow Killer.

High Bear considered. "I've changed my mind about him," he said. "We won't take him along with us."

"Good." Crow Killer shifted his grip on the rifle, seizing it by the barrel. "Shall we knock his brains out up here, or down there where his mother can watch?"

Big Nose also clubbed his rifle. "Yes," he said. "Where will we kill him?"

High Bear now shifted his rifle, too—but not to club it. He pointed it squarely at his two eager companions.

"Who said anything about killing him?" he asked quietly.

"You did. You just did!"

"Yes, you just said it!"

"I said no such thing. I only said we would not take him along with us."

19

"You said you had changed your mind! Don't lie!"

"That's right. I have changed my mind about taking him along with us. I'm going to leave him here with his mother."

Astounded, the other two braves pulled back their ponies.

"What?"

"Do you mean it?"

"I mean it. Don't you see my rifle looking at you?"

The three Sioux stared at one another. Big Nose, the realist, was first to break the silence.

"Listen, Cousin," he said to High Bear. "You are right about the children, even the little girls. We're not Comanches or Apaches. We Sioux don't go around killing little children. All right, let the children alone. Leave them here to wait for the Pony Soldiers. I agree to that. Crow Killer will agree to that. But the woman must die. We can't let her get to Fort Farewell and tell the soldiers where we are. That fort is too close to us."

High Bear knew this was the truth. He hesitated. As he did, a voice broke the stillness quaveringly. It took more courage than anything he had ever done before, but Red Fox knew that he must speak now, and he did so.

He pushed his mount forward to stand with those of Big Nose and Crow Killer. "Uncle," he said, "may I please have some words?"

High Bear looked down at his small nephew. In one way he was very proud of his sister's child. In another way he was angry with the boy for following them and adding his weight, slim as it was, to their traveling baggage. Now he nodded sternly and raised his sinewy hand. "You have ridden well. You have not complained. Speak."

"*Haho*, thank you," murmured the boy. "I wish only to say, Uncle, that it is not the way of Oglala warriors to be afraid of women."

"And I say it is not the place of sniveling boys to advise warriors!" snapped Crow Killer.

Big Nose began to agree with his friend, but High Bear cut them both off.

"Don't say any more," he advised them. "I have made up my mind. My nephew has a young head but with a very old tongue in it. Tokeya," he went on to the boy, "you go down there to that woman and tell her that we shall not harm her, but that we need her fresh horses. Tell her that we will leave her two tired ones for them. We will trade her Crow Killer's and Big Nose's ponies for her bays."

"Thank you, Uncle. What more may I tell the woman?"

"Tell her to put all three of the girls on one of our horses and ride the other one herself. You and the white boy go down there now. *Hopo,* hurry up."

"May the white boy keep his pony, Uncle?"

"Yes, of course. It is no good for us. Go ahead, now. Tell the woman she better be a long distance from this place, when my three other men get up here from packing the meat we killed."

"That's all, Uncle?"

"*Pte's navel!* What else would you have me tell her?"

"She is but a woman, Uncle. Suppose that she does not know the way to Fort Farewell?"

High Bear looked at him sharply. The trace of what might have been a Sioux grin turned the corners of his mouth briefly upward.

"You are telling me that you *do* know that way, eh, soft heart? You like this yellow-haired boy, don't you? You want to stay and help them, help him and his mother. Am I right?"

"Never!" Red Fox struck his small chest. "I am a warrior, even as yourself. The same blood, even. *H'gun!*"

High Bear nodded. "Well, warrior," he said, "if it proves

21

that the woman does not know the way to the fort, you are ordered to show it to her. *Hookahey,* now, out of here!"

"An order, Uncle?" The boy might have been smiling, also. "You are *making* me do this poor work?"

"Get out of here," repeated High Bear. "Someone must do it, and you're the only man I can spare."

"Me, a man? Ah, Uncle!"

The boy drew himself up, tightening his dark hand on the lead rope of the white youth's pony. "I go!" he announced dramatically. Then, to Crow Killer and Big Nose, with an imperious wave, he barked: "You heard the war chief! Get off those horses and give me their bridles."

The two outraged braves had only time to suck in their wind for whatever angry words they had ready to spit out when High Bear waved at them, too. But he did it with his Winchester.

"Yes," he said. "You heard the war chief."

His two murderous-looking henchmen had ridden with High Bear before this time. They were well enough acquainted with his temper to know that when his fingers commenced to drum and tap on the lever of his rifle, as they were doing now, a working agreement of sorts was indicated.

"*He-hau,* we heard, brother." Big Nose slid off his pony.

"A true thing," acknowledged Crow Killer, also surrendering his mount. "But remember this, Cousin, you are getting as soft in the head as that boy is in the heart. That's not good."

High Bear watched Red Fox lead the two Indian ponies and the white boy's pony down the rise above the arroyo, toward the ranch house. He waited until Red Fox rode around the stock corral and halted in front of the harness shed, and he saw the white woman look up in startled fear at the Sioux boy. Then he waited as Red Fox spoke to her and pulled aside his pony so that she might see her son Billy on the other pony. He still waited until, responding to a gesture by Red Fox, she looked up toward the arroyo rise and saw him, High Bear, with Crow Killer and Big Nose, poised against the skyline, watching her. When he was certain the woman was looking at him, High Bear raised his right arm, the hand held with the palm toward her. It was the universal Plains Indian sign of peace, and the woman clearly understood it. High Bear saw her glad wave of reply. Even though he hated the white people so badly, the young Oglala chief moved his own arm in response and felt a warmness in his red heart which he knew had no business there.

"*Ih!* Look at him!" said Big Nose disgustedly. "Waving good bye to the faded-hair squaw. Ha, ha, ha! Wait until I tell this to Iron Mouth and the others!"

"Yes." Crow Killer scowled. "Let me change something. He isn't *getting* soft in the head. He already is soft there."

High Bear paid no heed to the remark until he had seen Amy Lohburg unhitch the bay team and put her children up on the Indian ponies. Only when he was satisfied that things were going as he had ordered them to go, down in the ranch yard, did he turn to his comrades.

"The day that sees me soft in the head," he said to them, "will dawn many a long moon after you brave hearts have been at rest beneath the buffalo grass. There is a time to kill and a time to ride away. Wise men know this. Fools never learn."

The colonel's aide glanced up as the sergeant clumped into the office, dusty hat held apologetically at his breast.

"Beg pardon, Lieutenant. Like to see the colonel if I could."

"You can't. Tell me your troubles, soldier."

"If I could see the colonel, sir."

"Blast it, Fenton, when I tell you the colonel is busy. . . ."

Colonel Edgar Montague poked his friendly head out of the inner office. "Someone to see me, Lieutenant?" he asked hopefully. Then, seeing the sergeant: "Oh, Frank, hello. Come in, come in. How was the scout? Aren't you back rather soon?"

They went into the c.o.'s office and closed the door.

"Colonel," the sergeant said, "I *am* back early. That's what I wanted to see you about."

"Go on, man, go on. You know I've always got time to listen to a good soldier. Did you get to the Lohburg place? How about the Haraldsens?" No West Pointer, Montague ran his post democratically, using his noncommissioned officers sensibly, which was to say constantly. "Of course, you did. Wouldn't be back so soon, otherwise. Am I right?"

"Right, sir." Fenton told his story quickly, concluding with a frowning shrug. "I found a note on the Haraldsen door dated yesterday. They'd started for Fort Fetterman. Why, the good Lord knows. It's nearly twice as far."

Montague joined him in the frown. "All right, Frank. You got the Lohburg woman and her kids started back here, and you found the Haraldsens safely gone for Fetterman. Why did you turn back? I asked you to stay with those Indians if you ran across them, at least long enough to get a line on them."

"Yes, sir. That's why I turned back. I did get a line on them."

"How was that? I thought you left them east of the Lohburg place, where you found Dutch killed."

"That's so. But after I left Haraldsens' I got to worrying about poor Missus Lohburg and them little towhead girls. So I made a circle to check the ranch again."

"Yes, what did you find?"

"Don't rightly know. Tracks showed me where the Sioux

was there, two, three of them, anyways. But the woman and kids never left in the wagon I hooked up for them. The horses was gone and they was gone and the Sioux was gone."

"Oh, dear." Colonel Montague was a sensitive man. "I'm sorry, Frank. Well, you did all you could, man. That's why I sent you ahead of the regular mail rider. That stupid Dutchman! I should have put him in arrest and made him come in here to Farewell. Now those little children and that wretchedly mistreated Lohburg woman are. . . ."

"Sir, Colonel." Sergeant Fenton put up a hand the size and shape of a Virginia ham. "I still think we can do something for that poor lady and them kids. I think they're still alive."

Montague shook his head. "No, not very likely, Frank. If the wagon was abandoned and the team cut away. . . ."

"No, sir, the team wasn't cut away. It was unhooked. And there was two lines of tracks away from there."

Montague's honest frown deepened. "Now, let me get this straight, Sergeant," he said. "You believe there's some chance these people may be still alive and may be still trying to get here, as you told them to try to do?"

"That's half of it, sir."

"And the other half?"

"I want to go back out with some troops and try to find them."

"I see. And you figure that if you start back looking for them soon enough, you may be in time. Is that about it?"

"Exactly, sir."

The c.o. eyed him speculatively. "How soon would you say 'soon enough' might be, Sergeant?"

"I'll need time to saddle another horse, sir."

"Some troops to go with you, you say?"

"Yes, a few."

"How few?"

"Corporal Filister and one squad, sir. My pick."

"How do you want the orders cut, Sergeant?"

"Just a work detail, sir. There's some repair to be made on a couple of the sections of the wagon road, sir."

"Of course. Just a work detail. No officer needed that way, eh, Sergeant?"

"Well, I wouldn't want to be taking any of your young men away from their duty posts, sir. Not in an Indian time."

"You bet your life you wouldn't. Not you, Fenton. You're too sneaky smart. Get out of here. I'll tell the simpleton outside to clear you for a work detail and one squad. What kind of shovels do you want issued?"

Fenton saluted smartly. "Springfields, sir . . . Forty-Five-Seventies."

Red Fox had been sent to the Agency school at Pine Ridge. He had been made to go by the older Sioux. It was in their minds that a promising lad related to American Horse, who might one day be material for tribal leadership in his own right, ought to be taught the white man's ways, so that he might better be able to deal with the white man by knowing his tricks and the forked tongue with which he proposed them. Red Fox had done the council's bidding and done it exceedingly well. He had learned good English quickly and learned, additionally, that which he had been primarily sent to learn—how to think in the strange, cloudy manner of the white brother. No, not so much to think in that crooked way, but to understand the enemy who did use his mind in such twisting paths.

Thus, as he spoke to Amy Lohburg in the late afternoon of the long day's flight, Red Fox was very grateful he had studied so hard at Pine Ridge. It was suddenly most important to him that the brave mother of the boy and the sisters should understand the true meaning of what he had to tell them.

"Lady . . ."—he had called her that from the first—"lady, you take the little baby now." He himself had held the two-year-old before him on his own pony, but now he gave the child over to Amy and said to Billy Lohburg: "Boy, you get down and stay here with the women. There is something I must do back along the trail. I will return very shortly."

Billy slid obediently from his mount. "Sure thing, Fox. We going to camp here?" He had already begun to accept the death of his father and to lose himself in the pure adventure of the escape ride from the ranch. But now, as the Indian youth hesitated and did not reply to him at once, he lost his eagerness. "Something's the matter, isn't it? Come on, Fox. What you afraid of?"

"Boy," answered the Sioux youth, "you take the pony of the sisters, with your own, and lead them into that thicket by the stream. Hurry. I will talk to your mother a moment."

"Now, dog-gone it, just a minute, Fox! I ain't going to. . . ."

"Billy, do as you're told." Amy was almost harsh with it. "Red Fox knows what he is doing."

"Well, so do I!"

"You're the man of the family now." The Sioux youth was serious. "The man must take care of the women. Take care of your sisters, then, and your mother when I am gone."

"Oh, well." Billy was outwitted, not knowing how. He went with the girls, and Red Fox quickly turned to Amy Lohburg.

"I think we are being followed. Go into the grove of those trees with your children and wait there very quietly."

He wheeled the scrubby pony, then halted it.

"Lady," he said, "if we *are* being followed, it is Indians

27

doing it. And if it is Indians doing it, they will be those Indians with my uncle, High Bear. I know this because since leaving your ranch I have been going south in a big circle, to avoid them, as I knew they were trying to move northward, and so we should come to the Pony Soldier fort in a way far removed from the way the Indians of my uncle would be traveling. Now I am afraid we will not. It is a bad thing. You and the children must lie still as mice until I return."

"But, Red Fox, the leader is your own uncle. Surely. . . ."

"Lady, my uncle will not be with these Indians. These will be Crow Killer and Big Nose and Iron Mouth and the others, maybe. But my uncle will not be there. He said you might live, that I might stay and guide you to the fort. My uncle never lies."

"You think that. . . ."

"I think they either defied him or just sneaked away from him. But they don't come after us unless for one thing. They are afraid to let us reach the Pony Soldiers. I think they are coming to kill us." He saw the white face drain whiter still, and added softly: "I am sorry, lady. But I know you are brave. Good bye."

With that, and before she might object or think of further queries, he was gone. Amy Lohburg was left alone with her four small children in the late-afternoon stillness of a creek-side cottonwood grove, five miles north of the Niobrara River, thirty-three miles south and west of Fort Farewell, Nebraska.

Happily, or so it first seemed to Amy Lohburg, Red Fox was back within half an hour. Her relief lasted less than half a minute.

"Come a little this way, please," the Indian boy told her. "Tell the children to get ready to move on, but don't let them hear this."

Amy passed the order to her young ones—Billy commencing at once to help his sisters remount with the baby—and then followed Red Fox off a few yards.

"Lady," he resumed, "they are five who follow us. Crow Killer and Big Nose, the two who were with my uncle at your ranch, then Iron Mouth and the two others who were bringing on the slaughtered beef. They have all deserted my uncle and come after you."

"Deserted, Red Fox? But how is that? I thought your uncle was the war chief. Are you certain he isn't with them?"

"I told you he would not be. You see, lady, Indians are not like Pony Soldiers when they fight. Each Indian is his own chief. Big Nose does what Big Nose wishes to do. Iron Mouth rides which trail he will. Crow Killer stays or goes as Crow Killer decides."

"But, Red Fox. . . ."

"Lady, you must stop talking. I know my people. Big Nose and Crow Killer are bad young men. Iron Mouth is ugly, also. The other two are desperate to get away from the cavalry, so they, too, are dangerous right now. Do you see how it is, please?"

"No, Red Fox, I don't. If your uncle told them not to. . . ."

The Sioux youth straightened. His wide mouth grew hard. "Now be quiet!" he ordered her in sudden Indian anger. "You talk too much, now, just like a woman. You do as I say, or your little girls and your little boy will not see the soldiers at Fort Farewell. Do you understand *that?*"

Amy Lohburg understood that. "I'm sorry. What do you want me to do?"

"You shall see. Right now, the boy will follow behind me on his slow pony. You ride next, leading the pony with the three little sisters on it, as you are a woman and not able to do much besides leading a pony."

Amy smiled despite her great fears. The small Sioux had an irrepressible way about him. Honest, forthright, cheerful, yet realistic and simple of speech, he was a strange child to a white woman, and fascinating. White children of the same age—her own son was but a year or two the junior of the Oglala youth—would either be terrified or entirely unaware of the danger in such a situation as that which faced them now. Yet Red Fox spoke of it and planned to meet it with the calm and competent soberness of a man with work to do and no fear of doing it. It made the sod-house woman understand that in the Indian way of rearing children lay some secrets the civilized whites could learn to their benefit.

"All right, Red Fox," she told the boy. "You can depend upon me. I'm very grateful to you, I want you to know that."

"If I get you to Fort Farewell, or find some of the Pony Soldiers before that, then say thank you, lady. You save your breath for riding right now."

They went away from the grove at a bouncing trot, cutting across the creek. In midstream the Sioux boy turned his course upcurrent. Amy Lohburg and the children followed on their weary mounts, the animals having trouble enough to keep up with the seemingly tireless Indian youth, even though he now moved afoot, leading his pony to make sure of the way. The sunset faded; twilight followed swiftly, and still Red Fox kept to the rocky stream, leading Billy's pony, as well as his own, so that the other two mounts would tail them and not balk at the bad going. It was not until near darkness brought them to a long slab of sandstone, through which the creek channeled unbroken for seventy-five feet, that he led the cavalcade out of the water. Beyond the sandstone exit slab lay a low prairie swale, thickly grassed and overgrown with willow and alder scrub. Into this covert Red Fox guided his little party.

"Take the blankets off the ponies, boy," he told Billy. "Make a bed for your sisters. That is the man's job." He turned quickly, helping the stiff, nearly immobilized Amy Lohburg to get down. "You, lady, comfort yourself and the little sisters." He lowered his voice. "You must get them to go to sleep at once. Sing to them softly. Make them restful. They must be made quiet very soon, you understand?"

"You mean you're afraid the Indians still are after us? That they might be close behind?"

"There's no doubt of it, lady. Our tracks did not cross the little stream back at the first grove. They will be coming up the middle of the water, just as we did, looking for the place where our tracks come out on this side of the stream. If our friend, the darkness, will come soon enough. . . ." He did not finish and did not need to. Amy understood.

She swallowed with difficulty. Starting to say something, she thought better of it and swallowed once more, then went to work as Red Fox had suggested. When she had the girls safely bedded, she began to quiet their complaints of cold and wet and hunger. Billy helped her.

Red Fox also moved quickly and to a purpose. Snubbing each of the ponies securely and short to a sapling, he wrapped their muzzles with their bridle reins and told Billy to keep stroking them and whispering quiet talk to them in the Indian way.

"Tell them *ho-shuh, ho-shuh*," he advised. "That's Oglala horse language. They will understand it, never fear. I shall be back. You see that your mother and your sisters stay still, eh, boy? You're the warrior here while I am gone. *Ha-a-u?*"

"*Ha-a-u*," repeated Billy Lohburg, standing like a soldier at salute. "You betcha, Fox."

The Sioux youth nodded and was gone away into the early night. He crept along their back trail to the sandstone slab and the very edge of the creek. Here he found a tuft of tall grasses in which to lie on his belly and watch—watch and wait, heart pounding on the ground beneath him, small mind turning on dark Indian thoughts.

It was now a merely a matter of the race between three things: how quickly the full darkness of the prairie would fall; how quickly the trailing Sioux would loom up in midstream; how quickly the wet hoof prints of his pony and the ponies of the Lohburg family would dry away to nothingness on the sandstone bank, where they came out of the stream before this hiding place.

The race proved extremely narrow. The five Sioux horsemen came splashing and cursing their way up the course of the stream scant moments later. Red Fox carefully closed his eyes and prayed to Wakan Tanka, the Sioux Great Spirit. And warrior nephew of the fierce High Bear or not, his hunger-shrunken stomach grew smaller still at the guttural, Oglala words which now came to him as the Sioux halted their laboring ponies not twenty feet from his grass tuft.

"*Wagh!*" snapped Crow Killer. "Listen to me, all of you. Words will not catch them now. We've let them slip away and belly-down in the grass somewhere. Here is what we will do. We will go up the stream for a way, then we will divide into two groups. Some of us will come back down one side, some down the other, going very slowly. That way we shall jump them out wherever they are crouching and shivering. But we must go far enough up the stream to be sure we start moving above them. All right, *hopo,* let's go."

"Wait a moment," objected Iron Mouth. "I still say we must look through that swale over there, where all that willow and alder brush is. That looks fine to me. That's where I would hide."

"No." Big Nose was tired. He was short with it. "Crow

Killer is the leader. I vote with him. We can't waste the night looking under every bush between the Niobrara and the White River at Fort Farewell. We can go through that swale on the way back. *Hookahey!*"

There was another bad minute of cross grumbling, then the five shadowy horsemen started upstream, still swearing.

Red Fox slowly exhaled the old breath he had been saving all the while of the talk. He was dizzy, from holding it so long, and had to wait a moment for his head to clear so that he could stand up and run fast and without falling.

When he got back to the white woman, he found her still by the little girls, alert and ready. The boy was standing to the ponies, also faithfully, awake and brave.

Red Fox smiled at him and gave him a pat on the arm. Then he kneeled beside the mother. Tenderly he lifted the blanket and looked down at the sleeping faces of the three children. He smiled again and patted their yellow hair.

"I'm sorry, lady," he whispered, "but you must wake them up now. Be very quiet about it, please. They must not complain."

"But the danger is gone, isn't it? Didn't I hear horses going on up the stream? Oh, Red Fox, can't they just rest a little longer?"

"Wake them up, lady," repeated the Sioux boy. "A little longer is all we have to save them."

"You mean the Indians will be coming back?"

"Very soon. They said they would look into these willows when they returned. Our time is short as a heartbeat, and you are wasting beats for us."

"But where can we go now, Red Fox? What can we do?"

"We can run, lady . . . right straight for the wagon road which goes to the fort."

"No, I won't, Red Fox. The children can't ride any more

now. They can't ride fast . . . not without some rest."

"I will teach them how to ride fast without rest," the small Sioux told her. "You trust me, lady." He was cutting up his grass picketing rope into short sections as he spoke. "With its feet tied together underneath a good Indian pony's belly, even a white child will find that it is easy to ride fast without rest," he finished soberly. "Now you wake them up, lady, unless you want Crow Killer and Big Nose to do it for you."

It was a quiet night, clear as blown glass. The cold was that of a dead man's breath. The motionless glitter of the stars gave only enough light for the shivering rifle squad to see the back-flung wave of Sergeant Frank Fenton's upraised arm. The men pulled in their horses, crowding them closely together. It was not only cold, there in the night, but fear rode with the Fort Farewell patrol. Tensely they waited on the darkened trail, watching the two silhouettes in front of them.

"How far along are we now, Sarge?" asked Corporal Filister.

"About twenty miles. We should be into the sandhills any time. I make it some thirty miles yet to the Niobrara."

"Jings! Can I make a light, Sarge?"

"I suppose you want to see what time it is?"

"Yeah."

"Filister, what the hell difference does it make what time it is? It's black, it's cold, it's lonesome. That's what time it is. Go ahead."

The corporal struck his match. "Eleven ten," he said. "Lord, I thought it was three a.m. Lonesome? Sarge, it's spooky enough out here to goose-bump a ghost."

"It does get quiet." Fenton nodded. "I sure wish I knew what to do about that woman and them kids. We'd ought to have rode into them before this."

"We'd ought," added the corporal, "providing they ain't been caught up with from behind, or just plainly lost the trail in the dark, or providing you wasn't wrong in your reading of them split trails away from the Lohburg place, or a few other ors."

Sergeant Fenton shook his grizzled head. "Missus Lohburg's a strong, brave woman. She had a fairly good start, I'd say, was riding light, and she'd been over the trail before. I grant you it's easy to lose a set of wagon ruts in the starlight, but up to sunset tonight she'd ought to have been able to stay with the military road."

"How far did you foller them two sets of tracks away from the ranch, Sarge?"

"Not far enough, hang it. I was assuming one set was the Indians and headed north across the blind prairie, and the other was made by the woman and her kids hitting for the wagon road to the fort. I never did say I was halfways bright."

"Yeah. Maybe both tracks was Indian. Maybe they joined back up inside two, three miles. Maybe your Missus Lohburg and them little towhead kids. . . ."

"Shut up!" said Sergeant Fenton. "I'll do the maybe-ing around here. Let me be a minute. I'm working on a hunch."

The corporal shook his head sympathetically. "It was right gutsy of you to try," he said softly, "but we're too late. This is the third day them devils been on the loose. They cut down Dutch Lohburg, and that bloods them. They know that. They ain't got nothing to lose now. We know they was at the Lohburg ranch this morning. That gives them all day long to run down the woman and her young ones, even if they *did* get away in the first place. It don't figure."

"There's yet time. There's got to be."

"Sure, Sarge. Time to give them a Christian burial. And

we can't even do that in this pitch dark. Face up to it. There ain't no way we're going to find them, neither dead nor alive, in the blind black of this here miserable no-moon night."

Sergeant Fenton's burly shadow moved toward him. "Thanks, Filister, you just put the handle to my hunch."

"Huh? How's that, Sarge?"

"There may be no way we can find *them*," Fenton answered quickly, "but there's a way they may be able to find *us*."

"Sarge, you're all tuckered out. You're talking wild as a loon. Let's break ranks and hit the bedrolls till sunrise."

"Listen, Corporal." The homely sergeant's words were suddenly hard as flint. "We'll break ranks, all right, but not to go to bed . . . to go to work! You recall we passed a stand of cottonwood timber a way back? Send the men to gather up all the dead limbs and dry scraps they can locate and tote in. Make it on the double. Tell them I want a pony-load from every man jack of them. I'm going to build me a bonfire!"

"Good grief, Sarge! With these sandhills crawling with runaway Sioux? You want to lure in every homesick hostile within fifteen miles? You need a rest worse than I figured. You better be glad you're retiring next month."

"That's next month, mister. Right now I'm on plenty of duty."

"You'd ought to be on sick call. You're suffering."

"Filister, shut up and pass the order. If Missus Lohburg and the kids is still alive, the fire may bring them in to us. If they ain't still alive, it may bring somebody else in to us. It's what old Colonel Montague would call a calculated risk, soldier. Now hop it and rustle me up that firewood!"

"Yes, sir, Sergeant!" Filister said wearily. "That's my military weakness, sir, calculated suicide. All right, men!"

★ ★ ★ ★ ★

"Don't slow your pony, lady. Do not hold him back like that. Just let him run his own pace as he will. He is Indian-bred. He knows how to go the best gait. *Ho-shuh*, horse. Easy, easy."

With the steadying instruction to rider and mount, Red Fox waved ahead through the starlight to the darkling gleam of a prairie tributary. "It's wide but very shallow, lady. Everyone just ride right on across it, following me. Take heart, too, all of you. This little stream runs into the river that lies behind Fort Farewell. I know where I am now, I think."

Amy Lohburg tightened her aching limbs for the crossing. Her legs were on fire where they rubbed the pony's rough hide. Her arms felt like lead or iron, refusing to obey her, weighing a hundred pounds each. The children, young, tough, prairie-bred, were doing but little better. The baby, now carried again by Red Fox, was cold, weak in her movements, famished, and crying fitfully over it. Total exhaustion was near for all of them. The question remaining was how much farther their fear of the pursuing Indians might carry the white fugitives in their instinctual efforts to stay with the Sioux mustangs beneath them. Amy's reaction was to want to argue with the Indian boy, to resent his driving leadership, to refuse to let him drag her children one weary step more. But her urge to contest the Oglala youth's judgment had been entirely bridled in the chilling seconds she had hovered over her blanketed young ones back in the cottonwood grove where Iron Mouth, Crow Killer, and Big Nose had cursed their hunting luck and promised one another to search out the cottonwoods on their way back down the little stream. So she obeyed the Indian boy now, and called on her children to do likewise.

Hearing her do this, Red Fox smiled to himself and gave

the baby a reassuring hug. It made him feel strong to have a woman and these yellow-haired children of hers trust him like that. It made him know that he had done right to ask High Bear to let him guide the white people to the fort. He believed his uncle would be proud of him. With the thought of the fierce war chief, he turned his dark face upward.

"Dear Wakan Tanka," he murmured, "wherever you are up there behind the stars, please hear my prayer I send you . . . let me bring these white friends safely to the soldiers and then let me find my uncle, where he rides northward for the camp of Sitting Bull, and then let me go with him to Canada where I may live wild and free, as my mother and father before me, and give me, now, the courage and wily brain to outwit Iron Mouth and those others who ride after me and who seek to take the lives of these white friends my uncle sent me to guide. Thank you. When I am able, I will repay you. This is your child, Tokeya Luta. Please hear me."

If the Sioux Great Spirit heard the youth, He did not reply. But Amy Lohburg did.

"What is that?" she called to the boy, thinking he spoke to her. "I didn't quite hear you, Red Fox."

"Nothing, lady," said Wakan Tanka's child. "Just ride as I told you. You, too, boy," he added, to Billy Lohburg. "Wake up, now, here we go across the water."

He slapped his pony with the braided Sioux quirt, at the same moment digging his heels into its startled ribs. The little animal leaped forward, followed by the other mounts. They were all through the shallow crossing in a few snorting jumps.

Red Fox laughed, and slowed them down into their customary jogging lope, and said cheerfully: "That's fine, that's fine. Now just be easy and let me find that wagon road that I know is not far from here."

He lied just a little bit. It was hope that led him on, not

knowledge. He didn't know that little stream any more than he had known the one before it, where they had hidden in the trees. But if he told that to the faded-hair woman, or if her little ones should hear him telling it to her, then despair would be added to their fear. Red Fox knew that despair was a great enemy, and hope a strong companion. So he rode on forcefully.

But Amy Lohburg had lived too long in that country to lack sensitivity to its lonely terrors. When the children had settled down again from the stream crossing, she urged her mount up beside that of the small guide.

"Red Fox," she said, "how far have we come since the Sioux passed by us in the cottonwoods?"

"Five miles, lady, perhaps six. We do very well."

Amy shook her head. "No," she said, "I don't think we do." She paused, reaching in the darkness to find his thin arm with her work-hardened hand. "You're a wonderful boy, little Red Fox," she said. "I feel the same pride and love for you as I do for my own children. If we live, I want you to stay with us. Any family can use two men such as you and Billy. But you're still a boy to me, Red Fox, and I have learned to know when little boys are lying."

"Lady, what are you saying?"

"It's too much farther to the fort, Red Fox. You're lost . . . we're all lost. I'm so sick and shaky I can barely cling to this poor pony, and I know the kids can't hold on much longer. I'm saying I just can't go on, much as I love my children, *all of you*."

The Indian boy understood her last words. "Thank you, lady," he said. "You are strong and brave for a woman. You're a good mother, but I can't stay with you. My life lies with my uncle and with where my parents used to follow the buffalo. I was born wild and free. I know the land up on the

Red River of the North. I believe with my uncle, High Bear . . . I would rather die up there than live down here. I am an Indian."

"But, Red Fox, many Indians live with white people, and in peace, working together and staying together . . . the Nez Percés, the Cherokees, the Osages, the. . . ."

"Lady, these are other Indians. I am Sioux . . . Oglala. I am a horse Indian. We can't live penned up like cattle."

She started to tell him the Nez Percés were also horse Indians, that the Cherokees did not live penned up like cattle; she thought of the other tribes and people she had heard about, or known about, as a girl in the older settlements of the Mississippi Valley. But, looking at the haughty lift of the lean Sioux chin, the straight way the little boy sat on his pony, black against the gray of the starlight, she *felt* the difference. She seemed to know, suddenly, what it meant to be a true "horse Indian," a wild, free nomad who followed the sun and the buffalo on horseback from snow to snow, from cradle to grave. And she knew then, as well, that Red Fox was right, that he must go and find his uncle and live with him where the buffalo and the antelope and the elk yet wandered, and where men still rode horses across the summer wind, or raced them through the waving prairie grass, or skimmed them over the fording shallows of the clear plains streams.

She let her hand fall away from the boy's arm. "All right, Red Fox." Her tones were gentle, like a mother's. "Go where you will, but remember you will always have a home with the Lohburgs. We shall never forget you. Never."

"The way my people say it is this way, lady." The Oglala boy turned toward her, and she could see the gleam of his white teeth through the gloom. " 'The eyes fail, the ears grow dull, the words stumble, the mind fades . . . only the heart remembers.' "

"Oh, isn't that pretty!" cried Amy Lohburg softly.

The boy did not reply, for his body had grown swiftly tense and he was no longer listening to the white woman. They rode in this way for perhaps five more long-drawn-out minutes. Then Red Fox heard the distant sound once more and was sure of it this time. As for Amy Lohburg, one moment she and the Indian boy were riding knee and knee through the night, the first faint stirrings of real hope commencing to flutter within her. The next moment she, too, heard what Red Fox heard—wolf calls along their back trail. And in the following, third moment, the Sioux youth sliced the thongs of his plaited quirt across the rump of Amy Lohburg's pony and gave the same harsh treatment to the ponies of the girls and of Billy Lohburg.

"Hee-yahhh!" he shouted. "Now we really run, everybody!"

The children and their mother alike understood that the time for holding down the voices and keeping the horses going on steadily was now past. What remained would be a race between Indian mounts, theirs and those of the oncoming red men howling like wolves along their track. Clearly what had happened was that Big Nose and the others had, by luck, come up close enough to them in the night to hear their voices in conversation. On the open prairie, with no other sounds save those of horses, bridles, and saddles to overlay the human voice, that instrument holds a vibrancy of peculiar power. It had betrayed Red Fox and Amy Lohburg. Yet the boy would not give up, nor would he admit their true position.

As all the bone-weary mounts stumbled into their gallops, he brought his pony up beside that of Amy Lohburg's.

"Those are my friends back there!" he called to her. "They yelp like that when they strike a warm trail. They don't see us yet, though. Don't be afraid."

"Oh, Red Fox!" gasped the frightened woman. "We'll never make it! You and Billy slip away quick, you hear? As boys, you might get away. You're stronger. Give me the baby."

"Lady, don't make foolish talk. Just watch your pony. Don't hold his head back like that. He'll stumble and go down. That's better. You, too, boy! Good, good, that's the way."

He twisted in the dark, dropping his mount to the rear, letting it run beside that of the Lohburg girls.

"Eh, little sisters?" he said cheerfully. "Don't be frightened. Are you all right? I'm here. No harm will come to you. Hold fast!"

The eldest girl, the seven-year-old, quavered a reply that was more in spirit than words. The five-year-old sobbed a little, but Red Fox could hear the older child admonish her to stop it and hang on, as they had been told to do.

He put his pony again into the lead. Passing Billy Lohburg, he ordered: "Go back a little. Ride with your sisters. You're the man, remember."

The boy shouted back that he would do his level best, but wanted to know how far they were from the fort.

To this, glad the darkness hid the grimace that contorted his small face, Red Fox called out: "Not far, not far! We will get there. We will win the race. See, now, the ponies are running stronger than ever. Hang on! Ride hard, everybody!"

The ponies were running stronger than ever, he knew, because they were bred and trained to run that way. They would do it until they dropped dead. He did *not* know, on the other hand, how far they truly were from Fort Farewell and could only guess by *feel,* in the Indian way. That sense of prairie navigational instinct, seemingly built into the Plains Indian, told him that they were still a great many miles from the Pony Soldier stockade.

Their little Indian mustangs might last two miles, or three.

★ ★ ★ ★ ★

But three things were running on white man's time that night of the Fort Farewell pony race, and not on Indian time: Red Fox's incorruptible heart; Amy Lohburg's and her four children's sod-house toughness; Corporal Ben Filister's stem-winding pocket watch.

Fifteen minutes after the Sioux boy's desperate final quirting and shouting onward of the failing ponies and their tight-lipped riders, and with his own last request having just been made to Wakan Tanka to permit him to die in a manner his fierce uncle would approve, the Great Spirit sent High Bear's small nephew a very powerful medicine sign. Not one mile away, the sky was painted faintly by a reddening, then yellowing, stain. It began no larger than a boy's hand and built swiftly into a leaping flare of orange light and gray-white rolling wood smoke. *He-hau!* In the time and place, and by the fact that it was wood, not grass—this lit deliberately as a beacon—the fire meant but one thing to the small Oglala warrior.

"Pony Soldiers!" he yelled excitedly to his companions. "We have found the Pony Soldiers! *He-hau,* Wakan Tanka! *Hee-yahhh!*"

In the Sioux tongue, the last words meant a heartfelt— "Thank God, and let's get out of here!"—but Amy Lohburg did not need to understand Sioux or to translate those last words. She was a High Plains rancher's widow. What she understood was the first part of the Oglala boy's shout, the English part. With five known killer horse Indians riding up behind you in the black of night, unknown miles from the nearest fort, "Pony Soldiers!" was a language that needed no interpreter.

She beat at her staggering pony with her bare hands. She laughed gladly, a little hysterically, and she shouted aloud to her God and in her own wild language, no more English than Red Fox's. She was still laughing and crying, still urging on her little mount and those of her brave children, when the indomitable little brute stumbled for the last time to go down with its outstretched nose nearly in the ashes of Sergeant Frank Fenton's beacon fire. Behind her mount, the wiry pinto mare that had carried her two daughters sixty miles in less than thirty-six hours wobbled to a halt and stood, head down, nostrils belled, and blowing thin red froth. The animal stood long enough for Filister and Frank Fenton to remove the tie ropes that bound the girls' feet together beneath its belly and to lift the children hurriedly from its back. Then it, too, put its muzzle to the ground and went down, knees first, beside the other pony and was dead in a dozen fluttering heartbeats.

Billy Lohburg and Red Fox took care of themselves and of their mounts, as men should. The rough troopers, moved as only soldiers can be by great bravery and fortitude, had the martial grace to let the youths alone, save for a certain amount of hearty man talk. Moreover, they were soon enough busy with other matters of their dangerous trade.

For the following fifteen or twenty minutes Sergeant Fenton and his cursing squad of picked riflemen bellied deep into the fireside dirt, spraying Springfield lead at Crow Killer, Big Nose, Iron Mouth, and the other two outraged Sioux renegades, while Corporal Filister comforted Amy Lohburg and her dirty-faced, worn-out brood behind the shelter of their dead ponies.

No one noticed that, after bringing the baby to its mother in the first minutes of the fight, Red Fox seemed to have found himself a superior fort. Billy Lohburg glanced around briefly for him and then forgot the Indian boy.

As for the five Oglala tribesmen of the small guide, they soon enough lost their heart for shooting Pony Soldiers. None of them was military geniuses, true. Yet it took no war chief to realize, shortly, that they had been outguessed by High Bear's favorite nephew and were very much outgunned by the thrice-cursed Pony Soldiers of the big, homely sergeant who had gotten away from them at the place of the young cattle killing.

Very directly Iron Mouth said: "*Hopo*. That's enough. *Hookahey*, I'm going."

Big Nose spat into the dust, and nodded. "Me, too."

Crow Killer angrily cursed them and called them both cowards of the whitest liver, yet he beat them both back to where the ponies were hidden in a little gully. Within five minutes, the muffled sounds of their mounts' retreating hoof beats had faded away to the north, and the firelight shooting match was forfeited.

One Indian remained unaccounted for.

Even after Amy Lohburg had recovered enough to tell the story of High Bear's nephew and his strange devotion to her and her four fatherless children, and despite the ensuing anxious hours of hopeful waiting and watching into the outer darkness, the last Oglala did not reappear.

The soldiers and the little sod-house family stared the night away. The brooding darkness of the prairie gave them no answer, only staring back at them.

When morning came, the answer was the same, and it remained the same for all of the time that any of them would remember.

Red Fox was gone.

He was never seen again at Pine Ridge, or at Fort Farewell in far northwestern Nebraska.

The Rescue of Chuana

Niño stared off into the night. It was lonely in the Pedregosas. They were dry mountains lying but an hour's pony ride from the Mexican border. Nothing lived in them but thorny and horned things of the desert. No one came there. If they did, a man could see them from far off and be ready for them. The Pedregosas were Indian mountains and always had been. They were safe and certain shelter from the white man but, oh, they were a lonesome and homesick place.

Homesick? thought Niño. No, he wasn't homesick. He was heartsick. He wanted to see Chuana. He wanted to see her more than he had ever wanted anything in his life. But Agent Bullis had sent Chuana to the Indian school in New Mexico. Niño had stayed in the Pedregosas and wondered what the people at the Indian school were doing to Chuana, his *nahlin*, his young Aravaipa sweetheart. But the lonely winds and the long, hungry months had brought no news of Chuana to her fugitive Apache lover.

Niño had wandered the Sierra Madres of old Mexico trying to find a new life. He had visited the secret camp of his people down there—the seven Chiricahuas who had escaped from Geronimo's surrender in Skeleton Cañon, and the one warrior, Massai, who had gotten away from the train guards in Missouri and come home almost a thousand miles on foot and alone. But although they welcomed him and bade him stay with them, he could not bring his heart to forget Chuana.

And so, outlawed Apache or not, he had drifted back up to sit in the Pedregosas again and pine away for the Aravaipa girl.

In the end, the Chiricahua youth understood his sorrow was destroying him. It was the first month of the new year, 1891. Niño was cold and lonely and ill-fed, and surely the soldiers had quit looking for him so hard by this time. Why should he not go home a little now? Why would they want to hurt him any longer? Why not just get on that old ribby horse he had hidden in the rocks behind him and ride out of this desolate place and go home to see his people at San Carlos? Especially his friend Na-chay-go-tah.

With the longing thought, Niño stirred himself. He stood up, drawing his worn blanket about his shoulders. It was only a little over a hundred miles. In three nights on his old horse, he could be there. If he were lucky and found a new horse, two nights. He looked again northward, then nodded, saying something in Apache.

Going for the old horse, he already knew how he would ride it to avoid trouble. He would follow the Pedregosa trail up into the Chiricahua Mountains and through them, easterly, to strike San Simon Creek. He would go downstream, north by west, to the stage-line crossing where the old Mangas Coloradas used to hold up the Overland Mail Company coaches for a ransom of one wagon of shelled corn to pass safely through on the Tucson run from Lordsburg and El Paso. Then he would follow the creek and the military supply route to the Gila River and down that stream to the reservation and the *rancherias* of his people

When he swung up on the winter-ragged mustang, the aging brute seemed to sense that they were homeward bound. He went down out of the arid rocks of the Pedregosas, stepping along the secret Indian road over the Chiricahuas to San Simon Crossing as though he were four years old and a proud-cut stud rather than a pack horse gelding that would never see his sixteenth summer again. So well did he go, in fact, and so well went Niño's plan to avoid detection by boldly riding the Army's wagon-road route from the crossing up to San Carlos, that he brought his Apache master to the scarps of Chutanay Mesa, overlooking the *rancheria* of Na-chay-go-tah, the Pack Rat, just with the ending of the second night. Niño did not wait for the sunrise, but went down to the *rancheria* quickly and furtively, before the long purple shadows of the retreating dark should pull back to the mesa's foot, letting the sudden flood of pink and aquamarine daylight illumine each last pebble and prickly pear unsheltered on the barren floor of the Gila's wide valley.

His friend was at home and glad to see him. After the first exchange of Apache blessings and white man's firm handshakes, Niño did not use his host's tribal name again, but got at once down to the business that brought him here and to the good-sounding, direct use of old-time names.

"Pack Rat," he said, "I am sick and have come home to get well. Will you help me?"

The pudgy brave elevated his shoulders. "A minute ago, we called each other *schicho* and *schichobe*," he said. "Does a man say 'friend' and 'great friend,' only to turn away and cover his ears?"

"No, of course not. You will forgive me, old friend. I have been alone too long, and I am sick."

"You have said that twice now. Where are you sick?"

"Here," said Niño, pointing to his heart.

"I thought as much. It's that Aravaipa girl."

"Yes, Chuana."

Following the charge and the admission, there was a little awkward silence. It was plain that Pack Rat did not approve of young girls for old friends. But, as he had said, neither did

51

he use the word "friend" in idleness. His frown deepened.

"I suppose you're going to ask me if I know how to find her for you," he said gruffly. "Well, save yourself the trouble. Of course, I can find her. Was I not with the Indian police who guarded the Aravaipas when that fool Bullis had them sent to Fort Union?"

"It was that knowledge which brought me back to see you," said Niño honestly. "I thought about it for a whole year. Then I couldn't resist it. You're the only one who can help me."

"There's another," said Pack Rat. "If you have the courage to go see him."

Niño's dark eyes flashed. "You mean Sieber?" he cried. "You know where he is?"

"Naturally I know where he is."

"And he is well?"

"He's all right. He finds trouble getting work."

"That's because the agent dismissed him."

"Yes."

"The agent knew that would happen."

"Yes. He was afraid of Sieber. And jealous of him."

"He was wrong. Sieber was our friend, the best the Apaches ever will have."

"Sure." Pack Rat shrugged again. "But when you're a good friend of the Apaches, you're a bad friend of the white man. It isn't all Bullis's fault that Sieber has trouble finding work."

"You mean we are to blame, too?"

"Some of us."

"Like me?"

"Yes, you, Niño. Sieber gave you many chances. You always shied off at the last minute."

"I know, I know. . . ."

Pack Rat reached over, put a chubby hand on his friend's lean shoulder. "Well, don't look so sad about it," he said. "You can't help it if you are of the *cimarrónes* . . . you can't help it if you're of the outlaw blood. Some of us are, and some of us are not. You're wild. I'm not wild. That's the way Yosen planned it."

"He planned it a bad way, then," said Niño. "If a man is wild in his heart and not wild in his mind, he can't do what is right. Everything he does hurts either his Indian friend or his white friend."

Pack Rat nodded. "It's true," he said, "you've had a bad time of it. Not all your fault, either. But maybe we can make it different for you now. Something can yet be done. It's been a year and more that you've been hiding down in the Mother Mountains, and I haven't heard of a white killing or an Indian rape blamed on you since last spring. I really think the thing to do is go over there into New Mexico and get Chuana out of that white man's Indian school."

"All right, I'd like that."

"We'll go tonight. Is that soon enough for you?"

Niño's head bobbed in agreement. The first smile in many months lit his drawn face fleetingly.

"*Anh,* yes," he said softly in Apache. "Tonight."

A straight line drawn upon a map from the Fish Creek country to the old Indian town of Gallup, in New Mexico, stretches some 200 miles. Another straight line drawn from Gallup to Santa Fé stretches almost as far again. On the rough and arid surface, ridden by pony with the need constantly to avoid cavalry patrols and armed citizen-ranchers, the distance became considerable even for two Apaches to cover, undetected, in ten days. Yet that is the time in which Pack Rat and Niño came from Sieber's cabin to the Ramona Indian

School. It was, in fact, the nineteenth day of January, 1891 that the former drew rein on the juniper scarp behind the government establishment, pointed down through the gathering, bitter-cold New Mexican dusk, and said: "There it is, Niño."

The other Apache sat silently staring at the lamp-lit cluster of adobe buildings. There were many strong feelings in his breast at this moment, but he only nodded and said to his friend: "Yes, thank you. Isn't it strange, Pack Rat, how small it looks?"

"Maybe. But our minds work differently. I'm thinking how warm it looks."

"No, I mean isn't it strange how little a thing looks when at last you get right up to it? A thing you have feared and worried about for a long time? You know. Then, when you get there, it's nothing to fear or worry about at all."

"I'm still cold," insisted Pack Rat. "And, furthermore, you're wrong, anyway. We've got plenty to worry about down there. How do you think we're going to get Chuana out of that place?"

"I'll think of something."

"Yes? Well, it better be pretty quick if it's to come before my buttocks freeze fast to this damned saddle. By Yosen, Niño, I never felt a wind like this at home."

"It's a Mexican wind," said Niño. "It carries a knife."

They sat their ponies, shoulders hunched, thin blankets drawn tightly. Beneath them, the weary mustangs bunched their loins and stood, hump-backed, their manes and tails whipping like tattered black ensigns against the taut cords of their haunches and the ewe-boned tendons of their scrawny necks.

At last, Niño nodded and said: "All right, come on. I know how we must do it."

"Isn't that nice," said Pack Rat, kicking his mount around

to follow his companion's, "to have a brain like yours, Niño? Able to think of everything, and after sitting in the wind for only an hour, too."

"*Schichobe,*" said Niño, "we all have our special strong medicine. With me it's my fine brain. With you it's that wondrous nose of yours. Who else could have smelled out this trail in ten days only?"

"Thank you, *schicho,*" grimaced the pudgy San Carlos Indian. "It's a great comfort to be appreciated. It's an even greater one to know how strong we are. *Anh!* With your brains and my big nose, we ought to be able to get into more trouble tonight than any Indian since Geronimo."

Niño actually laughed. In his heart, the happiness was growing with each step of the little Arizona ponies down the scarped trail. Somewhere within that mushroom circle of friendly, twinkling lamplights ahead, Chuana waited. With his aching arms but another mile from holding her dear form once more, could a man show anything but joy over the testy comments of his faithful friend?

"Pack Rat," he vowed softly, "when the first man-child is born, he will bear your name."

"Yosen, no!" protested the other Apache. "You wouldn't do that to the poor little thing! Please, please. . . ."

But he was vastly proud, all the same, and he rode on behind his famous outlaw friend, sitting very straight on his tired mustang and thinking that to have the first-born son of such blood as that of Niño and the only daughter of Eskimin-zim called after him was as high an honor as might come in this life to a lowly San Carlos boy with beady eyes, a short, fat body, and a drooping, hound-dog nose.

"Now remember," whispered Niño, "grab her quick and don't let her cry out." Pack Rat nodded his understanding.

They lay up in the scrub behind the adobe wall of the compound, near the school well. It had been agreed that the seizing of the enemy for purposes of information had best be done by Pack Rat, for if the victim should recognize Niño, she might well have a heart failure or a stroke and leave them with a body to explain and no news of Chuana, or worse. "Sure," he said, "I know my business. But I wish you had let me take that fat one. The fat ones like to be grabbed. They giggle and roll a lot, but they don't fight much."

"No," said Niño, "she was too strong. Big as a horse. She might have thrown you."

"Hah! One time down in Mexico there was this Sonora girl who weighed three hundred pounds. She was like a wagon bull. Strong as Sieber. But when I got hold of her. . . ."

"*Shhh!*" said Niño. "Here comes a little one. No noise, now, *cuidado!*"

"Why, that's only a *day-den,*" objected Pack Rat, peering hard, "only a little girl, a baby!"

"Grab her," repeated Niño sternly, "and pull her over the wall."

The Indian girl came gracefully down the path to the well, carrying the earthen Zuñi jug atop her head. As she put it down to draw the rusty bucket full, Pack Rat slid over the wall, seized her by dropping his spread blanket over her head, bundled her over his shoulder, went over the wall again, and dumped her at Niño's feet.

"Get a hand over her mouth and hold it there until I have a chance to reassure her," he told Pack Rat.

The latter scowled, put his hand under the blanket. At once he yelped painfully and drew it back out. He damned her for an Aravaipa she-puppy, and tried again. This time he did not get bitten. As a matter of fact, a pleased grin broke over his cherub's face.

"Say," he told Niño enthusiastically, "this *day-den* isn't as little as she looked. By Yosen's big toe, she's got. . . ."

"You fool," growled Niño, "shut up and fetch her out from under that blanket. With you yelping one minute like a stoned cur and the next cackling like an old man with a young wife, you'll have the place buzzing louder than a smoked hornet's nest before I get to ask her one question about Chuana. *¡Callate!*" he cautioned, mixing the occasional Spanish word with the Apache and English that was the standard patois for agency and reservation Indians of his time. "At least, let me find out if my *nah-lin* is well and strong."

Pack Rat grumbled something in return and pulled the not-so-little Aravaipa girl from beneath the muffling shroud of the blanket. He held her close, one hand barring her mouth, while Niño patted her tousled hair and smiled at her in a friendly way. She did not seem unduly wrought over her capture and, indeed, appeared to be enjoying the situation to some extent.

"Do you know me, little one?" asked Niño gently. "I am a friend of your people. I wish you no harm."

The girl, a bright-eyed thing of perhaps fifteen years, nodded vigorously and pointed to Pack Rat's imprisoning hand while making protesting grunts and gurgles behind the press of his grubby fingers.

"Release her," ordered Niño. "She knows my heart is good and that I won't hurt her."

"I'm not worried about how good your heart is when it comes to getting hurt," said Pack Rat. "It's those damned teeth of hers that worry me. Ask her if she will not bite me again if I do as you say. I have but two thumbs, and she has already ruined one of them."

Niño put the question to the girl and got another emphatic

pantomime of agreement, and Pack Rat gingerly eased his grasp. The girl spat and rubbed her lips as though to clean them, fixing the unfortunate Pack Rat with a bayonet stab of her sharp eyes.

"Don't you ever wash your hands, little fat *coche?*" she demanded. "*Phew!* One would imagine, from your grip, how it is like to be enfolded by a bear! *Ugh!*"

"Well, I like that!" stormed Pack Rat. "Is that what they teach you here at the school? To take a bath all the time? To keep the hands pink and the feet scrubbed? Bah! See, Niño, how quick they forget the old good ways? Don't you know, girl, that water will weaken you? You'll get sick if you keep washing all the while. That's a terrible thing! If you weren't so young, I would take you away with us."

"I'm not so young," said the girl, interested. "Where are you going?"

"Oh, don't ask me," said Pack Rat stiffly. "I'm just a little fat pig. You said it yourself."

"Well, I like you, anyway. What's your name?"

Pack Rat glowed. "Na-chay-go-tah," he said.

"It's pretty." She smiled. "What does it mean?"

"Pack Rat," answered Niño, breaking in.

"It does not!" declared the small Apache. "That's just a name the soldiers called me at San Carlos. It has nothing to do with Na-chay-go-tah!"

"I like it even better," said the girl, patting him with her slim hand. "It fits you. I'm sorry I called you a fat little pig. You're really a fat little rat."

"By Yosen!" cried Pack Rat. "I won't have it. I don't have to sit here and listen to this ignorant Aravaipa field mouse call me names! I'm leaving."

Niño shoved him hard. "Sit down," he said, "and keep quiet. We've got business here. We've come a long way, and we must hurry even so." He turned to the girl. "You haven't said your name, child," he said. "How are you called among your people?"

"Many things," said the bright-eyed youngster. "But when I am good, they call me Hoosh."

"Hoosh?" said Niño. "That's a strange name. It's what we call the tart red berry fruits of the prickly-pear cactus."

"That's right. Exactly why my mother named me that, too. She says I should have a name to sting the tongue and prick the hands. That is, to be like me. So it was Hoosh she chose. Don't you think it fits?"

"Yes, I'm afraid so." Niño nodded soberly. "Now, Hoosh, do you know the daughter of Eskim-in-zim who is called Chuana?"

"Of course, I know her. She is practically my best friend. A little older maybe, but we like the same kinds of trouble. Why do you ask about Chuana? Who are you?"

Niño looked at her. "I thought you nodded yes, that you knew me, when I asked you just now. Did you lie to me?"

"Only to get a breath of air," replied the girl. "That Pack Rat grips you like a wolf trap. I don't mind, though. I rather liked it, I think. But, no, I don't recall your face. What did you say your name was?"

He looked at her again, and said quietly: "Niño." He saw her start when he said it, and it made him unhappy that his name should have such a harsh sound even to his own people. "Don't be afraid," he said, "please. I'm not what you hear. Those stories get tangled in the telling."

"Why, I'm not afraid!" said the girl, eyes shining. "I'm proud. Niño, here in New Mexico? All the way from Arizona? Why, that's a great thing. Chuana will just die. Her poor heart will fail her, surely, when I tell her this!"

"She is here, then!" cried Niño excitedly. "We have truly

found her. And she is well? Not sick in any way or hurt? They have been kind to her?"

"Sick? Her? You're talking about Chuana?"

"Yes, oh, yes. . . ."

"Well, hardly. Not Chuana."

Niño shook his head. "She was not strong," he said. "She was never really strong. I worried a great deal."

"Well, no. Maybe she's not strong like you and me and little fat Pack Rat here. But she's strong inside. Like a rifle barrel. You can't see her strength. It's rolled up inside her. Do you know what I mean?"

"Yes, I know. In her heart she is *palo duro*."

"Surely, that's right, just like hard wood. No, that's not true. Her heart is soft as soapstone. What I mean is that in her spirit she is like hard wood."

Pack Rat stirred uneasily, casting a wary eye up toward the school buildings. "My friends," he said, "I am very awkward to do this, but I must remind you that we can't *talk* that girl out of those adobe barracks up there. If you could rest your tongues and exercise your brains for a moment, perhaps we could get on with the business of stealing Chuana away from here. It's just a suggestion."

"Yes, and a good one," said Niño. "Let me see, now, what would be the best way to get at her from here? Hoosh, what do you say? Whereabouts is she up there?"

The tiny Aravaipa girl shrugged. "Well," she said, "if you want to make a lot of work out of it and perhaps get shot by the agent or the Zuñi police, why that's one thing. Go ahead up there and see what you can do. She sleeps in the big building, this way. I'll wait for you."

Niño studied her. "You haven't finished," he said. "Go on. It is we who will wait for you."

Her white teeth flashed in the windy darkness. "In that

case," she smiled, "if you stand here hidden by the wall, I will go up and get her for you and be back in ten minutes. That will include her clothes, some food stolen from the kitchen, the two Army blankets from her cot, and me."

"And *what?*" asked Niño, straightening.

"Me." Hoosh grinned. "Has the wind put dust in your ears?"

"Seize her!" hissed Niño to Pack Rat, and dived to trap the girl himself.

But she was entirely too quick for them. Niño went sprawling empty-handed. Pack Rat never got off his plump hindquarters. Poised atop the low wall, Hoosh laughed happily. "If you touch me, I will cry out like a she-bear in a dog fight," she promised. "On the other hand, if you give me your word that I may go along, I will have Chuana down here before you can brush off your shirt. What do you say, Niño? And, remember, those Zuñi police have shotguns. And I have a voice you will think came out of a split cannon muzzle. I'll count to three. Take your time."

"Wait!" gasped Niño desperately. "For the Zuñi police and their shotguns I don't give a pinch of tobacco powder. But I don't want to hear your voice. Not any more. Let me think!"

"Surely. Do that. *One.* . . ."

"Be a good girl, Hoosh. You don't want to come with us. There will be danger. Shooting maybe."

"Almost certainly," said Hoosh. "And any minute now. *Two.* . . ."

"Hoosh, please . . . !"

"Well, it's too bad, Niño. I always thought you were a great warrior. Good bye. *Thr.* . . ."

"Wait! All right! Have done. I'm beaten." Niño threw up his hands. "Go get Chuana. Bring the things you said. Also a

61

few for yourself. But not many. We will be four on two horses until we can get more."

The threat carried, young Hoosh sobered for the first time. Her slim fingers touched her forehead in salute of Indian respect. "Niño," she said, low-voiced, "you will not regret this. You'll see. Hoosh never forgets."

She was gone then, slipping off through the wind-whipped pepper trees of the garden, leaving the two Apache men alone by the adobe wall that shut off the Ramona School from the juniper and artemesia sage and the shadowy red-dirt ribbon of the escarpment trail that led due south and west away from Santa Fé and homeward to the twisted piñons and the palo verdes of Arizona Territory.

It was a lovely honeymoon trip, a little cold at first, or until they got past Gallup and started angling down into home country along the south-bearing Zuñi fork of the Little Colorado River. Then it warmed a bit. At the same time, however, the trail behind them did likewise. Pursuit, at first, had been nothing. By great luck there were no Apache policemen at Ramona, and the trailers among the captive Aravaipa bands of Eskim-in-zim and Chil-chu-ana at Fort Union would require a minimum of two days to get on the scene. School authorities, meanwhile, guessed that Niño had been the prime agent in the kidnapping. His relationship with Chuana was well advertised, and the added facet of Hoosh's being included in the abduction was accepted simply as evidence of force having been the method of the crime. But assumption and certainty are different steeds, and no positive identification of Niño had been arrived at up to the time that the Aravaipa scouts from Fort Union put in an appearance at Santa Fé. However, when the Apache trailers picked up the sign outside the school wall, they immediately held back and went into animated conference among themselves. Shortly they informed the white authorities in attendance—the school management as well as the sheriff and two deputies of Sandoval County (through which the escarpment trail led)—that they could make nothing of the sign except that there had been more than one kidnapper, no struggle, the mounts of the intruders had been barefooted and badly hoof-split, that one of them was a bay with black mane, the other—there were at least two—a grulla with mouse-colored mane and tail, that the culprits wore *n'deh b'keh*, Apache boots, that they were one bowlegged and fairly tall, the other knock-kneed and reasonably short—and that it did, indeed, appear that the abductors had been Indians.

This summation delivered, the Aravaipas stood looking blandly at the frustrated white officials. No exhortations of reward or threats of punishment could induce them to add another detail. When faced with the fact that they had already supplied a great deal of pinpoint observation and could certainly have followed the trail away from the school, it being plain enough for even the Indian Bureau people to see, Eskim-in-zim, who had come with his men, suggested quietly that, if the trail were so obvious to the good people of Ramona School, let them run it as far as they liked. He and his scouts had done what they could and must now return to Fort Union, as they did not wish the colonel there to worry about their being away so long.

It was now clear to all that Niño *had* been outside the school wall. While the deliberate delaying tactic of the Aravaipa, who surely had guessed Niño's part in the affair before ever they set out from Fort Union, had given the kidnappers a good start, it had also established positive identification of their fellow Apache. The telegraph keys got busy, and, as the fugitive lovers neared Gallup, the countryside was beginning to stir against them. It was then they swung south to hit the headwaters of the Zuñi and to strike down that stream toward home. From the third day, every rider on each distant skyline became an enemy. If he could be ridden around, all right, ride around him. If he came close and there was no avoiding a meeting, then he who shot first was he that rode on alive. These were the usual terms of Niño's life since the massacre on Kelvin Grade. But he was determined that this time they should not be forced upon him. This time, for the sake of Chuana and Hoosh and his dear friend Pack Rat, he must not let them put him in a place from which his only escape lay in killing those between him and freedom.

It was a deadly game. But with the skills and instincts sharpened by the two long years he had already played to its rules, Niño was able to lead his followers out of New Mexico without firing a shot. It was when he had gotten them a hundred miles into Arizona, safely onto the San Carlos Reservation and headed for home, that instinct, skill, and rare Apache luck ran out.

The lieutenant was not young. Neither was he inexperienced. He had been in the territories six years. Twice passed over for his captaincy, twice reprimanded for overzealous care of prisoners in the field, he was not burning to make a poor record better, but only to finish the present tour and retire with his two bars. He was, in a word, the wrong officer to be coming down the Fort Apache wagon road above Kinishba Ruin with Sergeant Rice, Corporal Schmidtlap, two San Carlos scouts, and ten men of E Troop, 3rd cavalry, at sundown of February 2, 1891.

The patrol was trail weary. It had chased a futile week after a band of Mase's Mexican Apaches up from Sonora to kill a few fat beeves on the American side. The Indians had made fools of the troops as they did each time a cross-grained officer of Beacham's type ordered a pursuit against the advice of his own Apaches. In this case, Beacham had overruled two of the best, accusing them of selling out to their wild cousins and ordering them put in arrest for the return journey. Thus, he had not only his ten troopers and two non-coms staring holes between his shoulder blades, but his brace of Apache trackers as well.

In addition, with their feet tied under their horses' bellies, their hands manacled, and their mounts ignominiously neck-roped to the crupper snap of the troop's lone pack mule, Josh and Nosey were in no position to overage Lieutenant J.D.E. Beacham.

It was Corporal Schmidtlap who saw the dead steer. The animal lay a pistol shot off the road, and in such a posture that it suggested something rather than disease or natural accident as the manner of its going.

"Lieutenant," he said, "that beef yonder's been fresh killed."

Sergeant Rice and Beacham pulled in their mounts. Rice waved back the halt to the column.

"Schmidtlap's right, sir," he said. "We'd best watch it. There's apt to be 'Paches about."

Beacham grimaced. "This close to the fort?" he scowled. "Don't be ridiculous."

Rice held tight. "Could be that's their thinking, sir, to come in so close we'd never think to look for them. I'd like to ride over and see."

Beacham frowned again, but nodded. "Corporal," he said to Schmidtlap, "you go. Rice, tell the men to stay mounted. We're short on daylight. Hop it, Schmidtlap."

The latter turned his horse and rode toward the downed steer. As he neared it, an Indian rose up from behind its body,

Seven

Stupe Wadell

The advance to the shack was not so simple as Waco had outlined. Both Waco and Jim were wary men, and this was the Big
Bend, where wariness paid dividends in continued living. Before
they reached the shack, they dismounted, and Waco pulled the
Krag-Jorgensen carbine from his saddle boot. That insurance
taken, Jim strode ahead, keeping out of line with the shack's
door, while his partner hovered watchfully beside the horses.

Before Jim reached the door, it opened, and a man stood
outlined by the light behind him in the doorway.

Jim called — "Hello!" — and came on, his caution
dropped.

Waco, too, advanced, leading the horses.

The man in the doorway stepped out and stood waiting.
"You the fellows that are camped here?" he demanded when
Jim came up.

"Yes," Jim agreed. "We're wolfin' along the river."

Waco, leaving the horses beside the corral fence, joined
his partner. "Howdy," he said brusquely.

"Howdy." The stranger was as brusque as Waco.

"Come in," Jim invited. "I see you built a fire."

The stranger stepped into the shack, Waco and Jim filing
in behind him. In the little room the man faced around. "My
name's Tayler," he stated. "I run cattle over this country."

"Pleased to meet you," Jim said. "My name's Barre. This
is my partner, Waco Ibolt."

Tayler made no move to shake hands. Waco crossed over
to the corner and dumped down the pelts he carried. The

66

Josh had said no such thing, but Beacham was suddenly smelling Apache blood and his captain's bars. If they could run the woman back to her sweetheart, they would have a prize second only to Lieutenant Gatewood's achievement in rounding up Geronimo. They mustn't shoot her now, whatever they did, but neither must they let her rest or quit running long enough to think.

"Keep after her!" he told Rice, sliding his horse up to the latter's, "but fire high. Just keep her rolling-eyed and running. She'll lead us right to him if he's around. Come on! By God, there'll be a promotion in this for you, Rice. Forward, ho . . . !"

The sweep of gauntlet and spin of horseflesh with which he led off the pursuit would have done credit to George Armstrong Custer, and so would the generalship impelling the flourish. Rice, an old soldier and hence badly frightened at the prospect of jumping Niño with only ten tired men, nonetheless rode jump for jump behind his excited officer. Schmidtlap, a less courageous, less dedicated man, let the three forward troopers dash by him, then followed with checked rein at the head of the remaining seven. The latter appeared satisfied with the gait, circumstances considered. Niño may have been out of sight for a year—he had scarcely been out of mind.

Ahead, the arroyo closed in. It would pass one rider for a distance of a furlong. Beyond that, it flared out to become a grassy flat dotted with large boulders and walled in by the flanks of the widened arroyo. Beacham, shouting in the lead, burst into this arena looking for the Aravaipa girl, Chuana. He found, instead, another Apache. A San Carlos. Medium dark and leanly handsome for a member of his squat, large-headed race. Very impressive, too, with his coarse black hair held in by its scarlet headband, his patched U.S. cavalry shirt

"You unsaddle the horses while I get supper," Waco directed, looking at Jim. "We sure overlooked our hand in not comin' to you before this, Mister Tayler, but mebbe we'll make up for it. We already got three wolves."

Jim went on out, leaving Tayler talking with Waco.

When he returned, the odor of frying bacon assailed his nostrils, and Waco had the Dutch oven on the coals. Tayler had squatted down beside the wall and was telling Waco about a big lobo that had been killing cattle almost at his headquarters. Dumping the Mexican saddle down beside the door, Jim joined the conversation.

The talk during the simple meal was brief and casual. Tayler spoke of range conditions, mentioned the fact that he had seen more wolf sign farther north than he had along the river, and suggested that the partners try trapping up in that direction. Waco assured the rancher that they would take his advice as soon as they had worked the immediate country, and Tayler told them of a camp up at the north end that the two could use.

The meal over, Tayler rolled a cigarette and made ready to leave. "I hate to eat an' run," he said, "but you see how it is? The moon's up, an' I'd better be goin'."

Both Waco and Jim Barre again pressed him to stay, but Tayler quietly refused. Accompanying him out to his horse, the partners saw the rancher mount and ride away.

When they returned to the shack, Waco spoke. "Seems like a pretty decent sort of gent, don't he?"

Jim nodded. "We should have dropped in an' asked him if it was all right for us to trap," he said. "I don't know why we didn't."

Waco curled brown paper about tobacco. Above the forming cigarette he looked quizzically at his friend. "I'll tell you somethin' you don't know," he drawled. "He's the gent the saddle. When I do, see if you can get your leg out. All right?"

Schmidtlap, speechless with fear, nodded. Niño put his rawhide muscle to the lift. Feeling the pressure ease, the corporal withdrew his leg and rolled free.

"Thank you," he said, weak-voiced, and sat watching the Apache, still livid with fright.

"It's I who thanks you," answered Niño. "You could have shot my woman over there, and you wouldn't do it."

"I couldn't," said Schmidtlap. Then haltingly: "Is she all right? Did they hit her?"

Niño shook his head. "No, they didn't hit her. She got away with my other friends while I stayed to talk with your lieutenant. I know him." He nodded to the dead Beacham. "He's no good. But I'm sorry about the sergeant. He was only a soldier. Only doing what he was told. I know how that is. You tell them at Fort Apache that Niño is sorry about the sergeant."

"You're letting me go?" said Schmidtlap unbelievingly.

Niño nodded. The soldier looked around uncertainly, eyes coming to rest on Sergeant Rice's body. "You're sure about him?" he asked. "He don't look bad hit. Maybe. . . ."

"In the heart," said Niño. "I had no time to be careful. I had to shoot him in the center." He glanced around at the gathering dusk. "You can walk to your friends," he said quickly. "We need these two horses, my friends and me." He took up the reins of Rice's mount, swung up on Beacham's fine sorrel. "You tell Josh and Nosey they were smart to sit still and say nothing just now," he added. "Tell them they will be even smarter if they keep doing the same thing. Can you walk all right?"

Schmidtlap tried a gingerly step or two, nodded again.

"Good," grunted the Apache. "Now we both go."

don't, he's the only one in the country who doesn't. I tell you, Waco, this is a funny deal, all the way through."

"Funny or not, he's the fellow that bought your saddle."

They continued to talk while they washed the dishes, discussing their recent visitor, considering various angles of the visit. The last dish dried, Waco made one final statement.

"Anyhow, he was all clouded up when we came in, an' it wasn't till that buckskin pie biter of yours tried to get in the door that he turned friendly. I reckon we got Monte to thank for him not runnin' us off." Having delivered this statement, Waco picked up the dishes and turned to put them on the shelves of the box cupboard fastened to the wall. "An' I'll tell you somethin' else," he said, turning from the cupboard. "We're out of coffee an' matches an' we're pretty near out of bakin' powder. We'll have to go to Gaskin's an' get some tomorrow."

"All right," Jim agreed absently. "We'll do it."

They rode their trap lines the following morning, Waco using the mule as a means of transportation. Both the horses, under the steady riding, were gaunting and showed that they needed rest or grain, or both. Accordingly, the mule was pressed into service, her rider decided by flipping a coin. When, shortly after noon, the two men returned to the camp, both were laden. Waco had two pelts, and Jim had taken two coyotes and a wolf in his traps. Both were frankly elated, and Waco indulged in a little crowing and a few I-told-you-sos.

So many skins to care for altered their plans. They had, that morning, decided that they would go to the Crossroads together, but now Waco vetoed that idea. He would stay and flesh the pelts and spread them, he said. Jim could go to the store for the supplies.

Jim demurred. He did not want to leave the work to Waco,

70

The Legend of Sotoju Mountain

"Hello, Barre," he said. "I didn't know you were in this country."

"Waco an' I came down to trap wolves," Jim answered, shaking Wadell's hand. "You're kind of a surprise yourself."

"I got tired of Carver City," Wadell said shortly. "Thought I'd try makin' an honest livin' for a while. I heard that there was a job open down here, an' drifted down to see if I could get it."

Jim nodded. It was on the tip of his tongue to ask Wadell where he had acquired the saddle, but he checked the words. Wadell must be working for Tayler. That would explain the saddle.

"How much do I owe you, Mister Gaskin?" Wadell asked, turning from Jim.

Gaskin added figures scrawled on a piece of paper. "A carton of Duke's Mixture," he said, "papers . . . the whole thing comes to three dollars."

"How do you like your job?" Jim asked as Wadell paid the bill.

"Huh?" Wadell turned. "Oh, the job. I haven't seen about it yet. I'm just headed there."

That was, patently, a lie. If Stupe Wadell had not been hired by Tayler, how had he come by the saddle? Jim held his peace. It was none of his business if Wadell lied, and it was none of his business who had hired Wadell. If the former night deputy didn't want to tell the truth, all right. Anyway, this — to Jim Barre's certain knowledge — was not the first time Stupe Wadell had lied.

"Here's your change," Gaskin said. "You go on south an' take the first road that turns off east. That'll bring you to Tayler's."

"Thanks," Wadell said shortly. "You doin' any good with your trappin', Barre?"

"Pretty fair," Jim answered. "We've got a few pelts."

"I'll maybe try that myself if I don't catch on with an outfit," Wadell declared. "Well, so long." He nodded to Gaskin, raised a hand in salutation to Jim, and strode toward the door. When he was gone, Gaskin made a little movement.

"What can I do for you?" he asked.

Jim still stared at the door. "What does Tayler brand his horses?" he asked abruptly.

"A hatchet on the hip," Gaskin answered. "Did you want somethin', Mister Barre?"

Jim recited his needs absently. He was thinking that Stupe Wadell had certainly left in a hurry. He hadn't stayed around and talked.

one day to ascend its mysterious heights and visit the *wakan,* or holy spirit, who lived there.

Tonkalla's people were a small band of the Oglala Sioux, a fierce, freedom-loving tribe of high plains horseback Indians. The entire life pattern of the Oglalas was woven about the fleet creatures that composed the pony herd. As roving nomads who each summer migrated to the high country to graze the herd in lush mountain meadows, who each winter returned to the lower valleys to find the sun-cured hay of the prairies, and who each spring and fall rode far out upon the great plains to hunt the shaggy buffalo, the Sioux had no other treasure to match their beloved mustangs.

Tonkalla knew this. As well, he understood the nature of his present duty. Each lodge, or family, of the band owned several horses. All of these animals were pastured together so they might be watched over more efficiently. It was the work of the young boys to guard the herd during the day, when the danger to it was less. At night, when the grizzly bear or prowling mountain panther might draw near, it was the old men of the tribe who sat in watch. Yet it was not unknown for bear, panther, or even wolf to appear during the sunlight hours. So it was the cardinal Indian sin for a pony boy to fall asleep on guard or, worse yet, to wander away from his post. Appreciating this fact, Tonkalla blinked rapidly, spoke out loud to himself, rubbed his eyes, shook his head. He even struck his legs with a willow switch. It was no good. He simply could not drive away the sunset drowsiness.

It was late in June. Even up there in the high mountain meadows the air was soft and warm. It was so quiet, so lovely, so peaceful there amid the tinkling of the pony bells, the whickering of the foals, the distant yapping of the camp dogs. Tonkalla's head fell forward. It rested, chin-tucked, upon his and no more uncompromising than the face of the man who held the gun. Standing there, Jim Barre had plenty of time to estimate Thad Gaskin, and to check and revise his opinion. The storekeeper, Jim decided, was a tough old jigger who would just as soon shoot a man as look at him. Then Ringold's drawling voice relieved the tension.

"Well, Jim," the ranger drawled, "looks like they've caught up with you. What you holdin' the gun on him for, Gaskin?"

"Tell him, Marilee," Gaskin said.

"I told him." The girl's voice was breathless. Taking his eyes from the shotgun, Jim glanced at Marilee. She had been running, and her hair was disheveled by the wind, and her cheeks were flushed. She was mighty pretty, Jim thought.

"What's all this about a saddle?" Ringold was grinning.

Relief flooded Jim Barre.

"Put down your gun, Thad," the ranger continued. "Jim won't run away."

Slowly Gaskin lowered the shotgun, and Jim Barre turned to confront the ranger and the girl.

"Now what about the saddle?" Ringold said.

"It's my father's saddle," Marilee announced. "I know it is. Ask him how he got it."

"How did you get it, Jim?"

In a few sentences Jim told how he had acquired the saddle. "I didn't feel like makin' a claim on you," he concluded, looking steadily at Marilee Clark, "for what I'd loaned your brother, so I just kept the saddle."

There was a small pause, then Ringold said: "I've known this boy a long time, Miss Clark. I've never known him to lie."

Bright red suffused Marilee's cheeks. She looked swiftly at

and quick. I promise you that after that you will have no more trouble wanting to sleep."

Mouse was not a bright boy like Fox. He took the willow bark dust and rubbed it in his eyes. The moment he did, he thought his eyes would burn into cinders. They felt as if they were sending out flames and smoke. Then they began to water furiously, which put out some of the fire in them.

After a few moments, when he could see dimly, he looked about for Fox. Strangely enough, the older boy had disappeared. Mouse frowned a bit, not certain what sort of friend the other youth had proved to be. But he was sure of one thing. Fox was not a false friend. He had told the truth. Mouse would have no more trouble wanting to sleep that sunset!

brought Father's body back, and he told Uncle Thad that Father had said to give the saddle to Dale or me . . . that it was valuable. Joe had reached Father before he died. Then Joe was frightened by all the talk of lynching by people that believed he'd killed Father, and about the mine that Father was supposed to have found, so he ran away, and took the saddle with him. Dale and I have been looking for Joe and the saddle ever since."

The three men exchanged glances. "An' Joe was killed down in a shack on Tayler's ranch," Ringold said slowly. "At least we think it was Joe. We never found a body."

With a start, Jim Barre recalled something he had heard in Carver City. He spoke quickly. "When Dale was killed, Stupe Wadell shot a Mexican that was wearin' Dale's belt. I talked to Bill Murry about that, an' Murry was sore. He said that the Mexican . . . Pancho Vigil was his name . . . had been teamin' around with a half-breed Chinese an' Mexican. Do you suppose it could have been Joe?"

Ringold nodded slowly, and his eyes narrowed. "That was probably Chino Joe," he agreed. "Dale could have found the saddle an' Joe both in Carver City. Maybe Joe went broke an' hocked the saddle, or sold it. But why was Dale killed?"

"An' there's a reason for that, too," Gaskin said dryly. "Howie Clark *did* find a mine across the river. It's wire gold, an' rich. There're men that have been tryin' to find it ever since. If Dale found Chino Joe an' got to talk to him, he might have got a line on the mine. It might be that somebody tried to get it out of Dale, an', when he wouldn't tell, they killed him."

"Dale's hands were tied," Jim said eagerly. "Waco saw that. An' he'd been beat up an' cut. He. . . ." He stopped.

With a little gasp, Marilee had turned from the men and was moving blindly toward the back of the store. In the ex-

Rainbow belonged to Mouse's grandmother. The grandmother, a crippled old lady named Ousta, the Limper, was the boy's only living relative. Her shabby teepee was the only home Mouse remembered. He loved the old lady deeply, and so he was even happier to see her favorite riding mare returned safely from its long absence. Ah, how delighted the grandmother would be when he told her of this surprise!

"Dear Rainbow," he now said to the ancient mare of many colors, "let me hold your mane and scratch that secret soft place beneath your lower jaw. Don't you remember me? Look, it is I, Tonkalla, the Mouse. Your trusted friend."

Rainbow grunted and whinnied. She bobbed her head, as if she did remember the boy. But Mouse could see that she was not as glad as he was, and he knew that something was wrong. He stood away from the little mare to see if she might be injured. She was not, but he did see what caused her condition of apprehension. Her udders were swollen and dripping with mother's milk. Rainbow had a new baby somewhere up on that darkening mountain, and it seemed to Mouse that she had come to the camp seeking help.

"What is it, little mare?" he asked softly. "Is your baby hurt or lost up there? You will have to tell me. It is two summers since you ran away to join the wild horses. You seem afraid of me now. You act as if you no longer trust in me. But if I am to help you, you must show me what it is that I may do for you."

Rainbow shook her mane and stomped the ground. She turned about and trotted off up the mountain a little way. There, she looked back at the boy and stomped again. When he did not move, she whinnied sharply and wheeled away once more up the mountainside.

Then it was that Mouse understood what she was telling him: she wanted him to follow her! Yet what could he do? As dismembered saddle with the handle of his screwdriver and looked at Marilee.

"Nothin' here," he said. "Are you sure that this was your daddy's saddle?"

The girl nodded. "I'm sure of it," she said. "I remember the carving on the fenders and the *tapaderos,* and I made those spur tracks across the seat myself. I fell off one time, and my spur rolled across. There used to be silver ornaments on the skirts, and there was a big silver plate on the horn, but they're gone now."

"Likely Chino Joe took them off an' sold 'em," Ringold commented. "They're sure gone. Nothin' but rawhide on the horn."

This was true. The big, pie-plate horn was covered with rawhide, and rawhide was wrapped around its shank and the A of the fork.

"Well," the ranger captain continued, "I've torn the saddle apart. You can put it back together, Jim." He looked at Marilee, his long face kindly. "Reckon it's a washout, girl."

Marilee nodded.

Gaskin placed his arm around her shoulder "Don't feel too bad," he said.

"I . . . I think I'll go home, Uncle Thad." Marilee looked up at the storekeeper.

Jim turned from the work of reassembling the saddle. "I'll leave this here for you," he said. "It was your daddy's. . . ."

"No," interrupted Marilee. "Dale left it with you. I want you to have it. I'm sorry about what I said. I recognized the saddle the minute I saw it, and just for a moment I thought. . . ." She broke off, slipped from beneath Gaskin's arm, and, with no other word, went toward the door. Uncomfortably the men watched her leave.

"She's been countin' on learnin' a lot when she found the

Chapter Three

When a herd boy was on guard, he was given a weapon. It was always the same weapon, passed from one boy to another when the guard was changed. It was a heavy and ancient trade musket bought with beaver pelts at Fort Bridger long ago. Loaded from the muzzle, it was fired by a flintlock, and the hole in the end of its barrel would admit Mouse's finger easily. The Indian boys poured everything down its rusted throat, scrap iron, lead, even rocks on top of the gunpowder. It went off with a horrendous roar and made an awesome wound—if it struck anything. But it was almost impossible to hit anything smaller than a teepee with it, even when it went off, which it seldom did when fired.

The herd boys called the rifle Old Caniyassa, from the Oglala word meaning to fail over and over again. It was this doubtful weapon that Mouse now panted and struggled to carry up the mountain behind Rainbow. The boy was thinking mostly of meeting Mato, the great grizzly bear, with such an ancient musket. The thought hardly reassured him. This was Mato's mountain. To be upon it after dark was a bad thing, by itself. But to be there with only Old Caniyassa for protection—*ai!* that was really frightening.

Mato was not like most grizzly bears, which would leave an Oglala boy alone if the Oglala boy left them alone. For this great bear bore a grudge against the band of Iron Road. He was an old bear with a long memory. What it was that he remembered about the Oglalas had made him a legend among the Sioux of all that land. Mouse knew the story well.

Many summers gone, some Oglala young men were out hunting upon this same mountain of the rainbow gorge. Near the end of the day they came upon a yearling grizzly bear cub of a strangely dark color. He was remarkable also for his great size. Upon seeing this young bear, the young men determined to have some practice with him at throwing their ropes.

They soon surrounded the bear. They commenced whipping him with doubled ropes. They were getting him angry, making him stand erect and paw at them. When he did this, a rope at once settled on his right paw, and grew tight. The warrior who held the rope ran to his pony. Mounting, he dragged the helpless young bear along on the ground by one paw. Other ropes were flung onto him by other young men. Soon he was stretched helplessly, caught by all four paws. In this shameful condition he was hauled down the mountain and into the Indian camp. Being but a young bear, he was terrified. Yet he made no outcry. The Oglalas gave him little credit for his courage. They teased and tormented him past all reason.

Mouse scowled angrily as he thought of the old story. Indians were supposed to love animals, but they could be very cruel, it seemed. When night fell, the People made a big fire, deciding they would roast the young bear. Bear meat, especially grizzly bear meat, was esteemed by the tribe. The warriors believed that it gave them the bravery of the bear. The mothers thought that the bear meat would give their babies the strength of grizzlies. All this meant the end for poor Mato. Mouse wiped his eye as he thought of it.

The Oglalas put the big cub in a bear cage made of pine saplings driven into the earth and roofed with more poles bound with rawhide. The door was of iron, stolen from an old

I think we'll do all right where we are for a while."

"You get around an' talk to people," Ringold ordered. "Talk to these Mexicans an' learn what you can. You haven't run across anythin' yet?"

"Nothin' for certain," Jim answered. "You'll know as soon as we do."

"All right," Ringold returned. "Just stay the way you are for a while, then. But don't let this other business sidetrack you. You keep your eyes an' your ears open, an' tell me what you learn."

He was through with his saddling then and ready to go. Ringold shook hands with him. "Don't forget," the captain warned. "Don't go back on me now, you an' Ibolt."

"We won't forget," Jim assured. "An' we won't go back on you."

The afternoon was waning as Jim Barre, the flour sack containing his purchases bumping against his leg, rode back toward the camp and Waco. There were many things to occupy his mind as he rode south. First was the warning that Ringold had given him. Jim Barre, from past experience, knew how the Texas Rangers worked. They moved into a country where there was trouble, and that trouble was cleaned up. But this time Ringold was there to prevent trouble, and so he needed spies. The way to do that was to make a great many acquaintances and friends, particularly among the natives — make them believe in you. Then a word here, a hint dropped there, a rumor heard and followed out, and a man had information to report.

But that sort of thing took time, and, too, a man had to have a good reason to be in a country, or else he aroused suspicion. The way to get the necessary extra time was to run fewer traps. That was easy. But a wolfer that didn't trap would be an object of conjecture and suspicion. Waco and the cage and grunted in a soft whine to the old woman. She put her hand into the cage to stroke his great head. He did not bite her, but only grunted softly again.

She put her wrinkled hand upon the iron bolt that held the heavy door closed. She felt her spirit soar.

"Mato," she whispered, "I am giving back to you your life which my people would take. *Hau, cola!* It is wrong for wild free things to be placed in a cage."

With those words the old woman swung open the iron door and permitted the young bear to go free.

Mato came out of the cage with such a blundering rush that he knocked the old woman down. She fell very hard against the iron door and damaged the bone in her hip. For many months after, she lay in pain and could not walk. When she did arise at last, she could only hobble about with a twisting limp. The People were still angry with her and insisted to her that Mato had tried to harm her as a reward for her foolish generosity in freeing him. They all laughed at the old woman and told her she was crazy in the head. For this, however, they did not hold her to account, being gentle with those who could no longer think clearly. For her part, she never believed them about the bear. She knew Mato had not meant to harm her. He had only been fleeing for his life.

The People gave the old lady a new name in honor of her adventure. They also warned her sternly not to set free any more good bear dinners or things would not go so pleasantly with her next time. They did not mean it, of course. Among the Sioux respect for the old is a law of the tribe, as is love for the young. So about all the old lady really gained from her rude experience with the huge grizzly captive was her new name. Yet that was a very important matter to Tonkalla, the Mouse. For the name was Ousta, the Limper, the name of his own beloved old grandmother.

Tayler, what was he doing riding Jim Barre's old saddle?

The trail that led to camp branched off the road here, and Jim turned Monte toward it. He hurried now, for dusk was approaching. Monte, knowing that he was homeward bound where he would get rid of his load, hurried along, trotting over the trail. Jim thrust the maze of thoughts back in his mind, shelving them. He would thresh the whole thing out with Waco after he reached camp. And when Waco heard the story, he would probably arrive at the same conclusion that Jim Barre had reached — that the Lemoines might be connected with the killing of Dale Clark, just as they were implicated in the murder of Chino Joe.

But there was someone with the Lemoines. There had been four horses along the corral fence at the old cow camp, and Jim had glimpsed someone inside the door when the sudden battle began. Surely there had been others with the Lemoines in the camp the night that Chino Joe had died. The whole thing, Jim told himself savagely, revolved about a gold mine — a fabulous lost mine that Marilee's father, old Howie Clark, was supposed to have discovered. Dale Clark, searching for a clue to that mine, was dead, murdered. Chino Joe, perhaps possessing a clue, was also dead. And there were living men who would kill again, just on the chance of getting track of that mine, when possibly there was no mine at all. Gold and the things men would do for it!

Between the ridge top and the camp, the ground was fairly clear of brush. Dusk had come, and down below him Jim could see the dark bulk of camp and corral. Presently the moon would rise, and all the little valley would be flooded with silver, but now it lay in shadow, and, amidst the shadow, a spot of light glowed. Waco had the door open, and the firelight cast a welcome glow. Lifting his voice, Jim called: "Hiyah . . . Waco!"

The neck fur of his roach, stiff with anger, rippled like prairie grass before the cyclone wind. His small, glinting eyes seemed on fire with his hatred of Mouse's people. His enormous body loomed as big to the terrified boy as that of a buffalo bull. And now this monster of the mountain night was dropping on all fours once more and shuffling toward him!

He came fast, as bears do with their awkward, lumbering gait. Mouse tried to cry out. He attempted to raise Old Caniyassa to fire. He commanded his legs to run away. But it was too late. Mato was so close to him that he felt the panting of his rank breath. He smelled, too, the musty odor of the great furry body. The snarl on the huge black face of the animal seemed to tell Mouse that the bear knew him for an Oglala, that he was reminding Mouse that he was the same young bear cub his people had tormented those many years ago. When this thought came to the boy, a second thought came, also.

"Mato!" he cried suddenly. "You should not bite me. I am your friend!"

At the sound of his voice the great bear stopped. He stood staring at the small figure in front of him, head held to one side like that of a curious dog.

"Mato," the boy pleaded, "it is I, Mouse, the grandson of Ousta, the old woman who freed you from the cage. Here. Smell my hand. You will know I am her grandson then."

It was a rash act, one showing the peculiar faith of Indians in their relationship with the things of the wild. Yet, after a moment's stillness, Mato made a soft sound in his chest and put out his muzzle and touched the boy's hand. He moved his nose over the hand, snuffling deeply of its scent. Mouse stood there, heart hammering.

Mato quit sniffing his hand. Uttering another rumbling—"*Woofff!*"—he stood up on his rear legs. He stared over the gunflame. One more shot in his Colt.

Then from the shack Waco yelled: "They're outside, Jim. Outside! Three of 'em!"

mare and growling in a muttering way to himself. The boy was glad he took Rainbow as he did. Bears had to eat, but it would have been a hard thing for Mouse to watch Mato begin that particular meal. Even as it was, he felt like weeping. Yet he had the little foal to care for, and that would take all of his courage.

The moon was rising to shed its ghostly light. The night wind whistled eerily through the dark places. If Mouse did not make haste, the spirits of the dead might come out of the earth and capture him. He must get down off the mountain before such a fearful thing could occur.

He freed the foal from the rocky crevice. With his long, wobbly legs and being only some few hours old, the son of old Rainbow proved most difficult to manage on the trail, but in some manner Mouse kept him going downward. They both fell many times. Yet each time the foal would nuzzle the boy's ear and whicker softly to him, and Mouse would rise up once more and start on, feeling strong as any warrior of full battle age. In this way they came at last to the camp.

Later, when both had been warmed and fed in the buffalo-hide teepee of the old grandmother, Mouse commenced to believe he was really a warrior. The old lady spread the tale of his conquest of mighty Mato all about the camp. Many of the People came to hear the remarkable account. Even Iron Road, the stern chief, came to the teepee of Ousta, asking to hear from the boy's own lips the details of the great victory.

Mouse obliged him with large pleasure. But when he had finished the tale, Iron Road only nodded and picked up Old Caniyassa from where his wandering herd boy had leaned it against the wall of the grandmother's teepee.

"And would you have fired the rifle at Mato, had he not obeyed your command and stopped short of harming you?" he asked the proud youth.

down, over by the corral. One had taken a horse and pulled his freight. That left one more. Jim Barre resumed his cautious circling. The remaining attacker was behind the shack, and to the east the edge of the rising moon showed above the ridge. Jim hastened. He wanted to gain his vantage point before the moon came up. Then, with moonlight, he would make it mighty tough on that jasper. He'd learn that boy to suck eggs.

Evidently the man behind the shack had the same idea as Jim's, but in reverse. There was a minute of silence, during which time Jim moved about ten long yards. Then, again, there was the sudden rattle and clatter of a moving horse. Jim straightened up and swore. The shack was between himself and the horse. He had come too far. And this last rider was making tracks toward the east, making them mighty fast.

Half the moon was over the ridge now, and there was light on the opposite slope. Gun ready, Jim reached the dark side of the camp and slid along the wall.

"Waco," he said, low voiced.

Wrathfully his partner answered. "Come in here, dang it! Let me loose!"

Still cautious, Jim Barre slid along the side of the shack, reached the door, and looked around the edge. Waco, hands and feet tied, lay prone in front of the fireplace. Jim stepped in through the door, slammed it shut, and went hastily to his partner.

The butcher knife from the table sliced through the softly braided pigging strings that bound Waco's wrists and ankles. Righted, the little man sat on the bench while Jim washed a gash on his head, cut away hair, and exposed the ragged lips of the wound. And while his partner worked, Waco talked.

"A dog-gone Mexican!" he raged. "He came in here about two hours after you'd left. Rode in just as pert as you please. I was fleshin' a hide, an' he got off his horse an' come over to watch. Friendly as all get out. We talked along, an' I was pumpin' him, an' all of the time it was Agapito de Griego. First thing I knew, he'd throwed down on me.

"'*Manos alta, señor,*' he says. Jumpin' Jehoshaphat! I'd left my gun belt on the table. There wasn't nothin' for me to do but put my hands up."

Jim, delving into a pack box, brought out the bottle of horse liniment and uncorked it. Waco, seeing what was about to happen, broke off his tirade to protest: "Don't put that stuff on me, Jim. It burns like blazes."

"Got to stop the bleedin'," Jim countered, and advanced with the bottle.

"My gentle Nellie!" Waco swore, as the liniment bit and burned.

"An' then what happened?" Jim demanded

"Then them two Lemoines come trailin' in," Waco continued. "They was supposed to meet de Griego at that other camp, from what they said, an' they was pretty sore. Them Lemoines are tough. They was all for beefin' me, but de Griego wouldn't have it. They jabbered a while, an' then tied me up. The Lemoines are runnin' guns, Jim. That's what they met de Griego about. He's got a camp on the other side of the Río, an' he come over to fix it up about a shipment. They talked about that, an' then one of the Lemoines kicked me an' asked me where you was. I told him to go to the devil. They talked a while where I couldn't hear 'em, an' then one of 'em come back an' kicked me again.

"'We'll wait for that pardner of yours,' he says. 'We want his saddle.' About that time de Griego come in again. I didn't know how the hell I was goin' to warn you. What happened outside?"

"I came down the trail an' had reached the corral, when

nothing in particular. His name was Pesla, meaning Bald Head. He had been given the name when all his hair fell out from the spotted fever. He looked very strange, and the other children avoided him. Mouse had no reason to do so. His grandmother was called crazy, and he was named a liar. So he had a friendly eye for Pesla, as fellow outcasts are wont to have for one another.

"Good morning, Bald Head," he greeted the younger boy pleasantly. "What are you drawing there in the dirt with that stick?"

"A picture of you, Mouse," the other replied. "Come and see it."

Mouse squatted beside him. His eyes grew wide. What a fine picture! It showed him fighting Mato up on the mountain. There were Rainbow, the foal, everything.

"Bald Head," he admitted, "I had no idea you drew so beautifully."

"Neither did I." Bald Head shrugged modestly. "But thank you, Mouse. You are always kind to me."

"Of course," agreed Mouse. "How would you like to come over to my grandmother's teepee and help me think of a name for Rainbow's foal?"

"*Ai!* That would be too kind. Might I touch the little horse, pat his head one time, or three times?"

"Four times if you like. Come on."

Together the two boys dashed happily across the camp. But when they arrived at the teepee, they found a large crowd gathered about it. They knew at once that something bad had happened, because the squaws were beginning to wail.

The young men had come back down from the mountain, and two of them lay silently across the backs of their ponies. The young men had found Mato at his breakfast, even as

"You done a thorough job on him," the little man commented, picking up the gun.

"Monte, shyin' the way he did, was lucky," Jim said. "These fellows are the devil on clubbin' a gun, Waco. That's what they used on Chino Joe, an' that's what they used on us."

"They'll get a few more lessons, an' we'll learn 'em that a gun's to shoot with," Waco promised grimly. "That is, if they live. This 'un will never learn nothin' any more."

"There's Monte up on the slope with Oscar an' the mule," Jim drawled. "I'll get him an' unsaddle. He just about saved my life."

Waco slid the bolt of the Krag back and forth, and clicked the safety. "I'll go along with you," he announced. "You stayed a mighty long time at the Crossroads, Jim."

"Had a lot of things happen myself," Jim informed him. They walked side by side, away from the corral to where the horses stood on the moonlit slope. "I'll tell you why by an' by. Right now, I've got an idea."

"An idea?"

"Yeah." Jim's voice was thoughtful. "This Agapito de Griego came over here to talk about gettin' some guns from the Lemoines. That's what you said, isn't it?"

"Yeah." There was no comprehension in Waco's tone.

"Ringold," Jim continued slowly, "is mighty anxious about guns an' such. An' we promised to help him out."

"So?" Waco said.

"So you heard de Griego say that he had a bunch of his men on the other side of the creek." Jim spoke firmly now. "I think I'll try to slip over there an' scout 'em. Mebbe we can't tell Ringold where the guns are comin' from, but I might learn where they're goin'."

There followed a little silence. The men had stopped, and

But the boy shook his head. "Grandmother," he insisted, "you know what shivering I mean. It was no morning chill of which I speak. I believe that Yunke Lo touched me with his cold hand."

At this the grandmother looked at him a long time. At last she nodded. "Yes," she said, "Yunke Lo was there. But he did not touch you. You only felt his cold breath. We all did."

"Oh?" said Mouse. "Then you think he did not beckon me?"

"Of course, he did not!" exclaimed the old lady. "Forget him, do you hear? I have met him many times in my long life, and he has not harmed me. Yunke Lo is like the moon, the sun, the stars. He is always with me. Yet we do not fear the other things, why should we fear him? Now don't worry any more. Poof! Old Yunke is no more dangerous than that rusted rifle you carry to guard the herd. Indeed, much less so. Go and feed that foal now. Life, boy, that is what counts, not the other. *Hopo!* Get out of here and take care of your new pony!"

The boy obeyed her. But he was very swift in the way he dodged through the teepee door and very fast of foot as he ran through the darkness to where he had tied the foal with their old pack mule, Sunsunla, for a companion. After all, he told himself, his grandmother was bent nearly double with the weight of her many winters. It was easy for her to be brave about Yunke Lo.

Ten

Night Scouting

Jim did not want the smaller man to go along on this expedition, but Waco was adamant, and short of tying him again there was no way to dodge his company. Jim waited while his partner saddled and put the Krag in his saddle boot, and then, side by side, they rode across the clearing and toward the river.

"De Griego helped himself to my six-shooter," Waco announced when they were halfway to the southern boundary of the clearing. "So I just took Lemoine's." Glancing at his companion, Jim could see the heavy belt sagging about the little man's waist. "An' I'm goin' to have to put galluses on it to keep it from comin' down around my knees," Waco concluded. "Lemoine must have been a couple of yards around the middle."

They reached the brush then and entered the trail that led down to the river. Jim made no comment. Now was not the time to talk. Now was the time to peer through the moonlight, to examine every shadow, every rock, every brush clump.

Monte walked slowly. The horse was tired. They were, Jim thought idly, going to have to do something about their horses. Both Monte and Oscar were getting too much riding. Waco, a trifle in the lead, stopped the grulla suddenly.

"Here we are," he said in a low voice. "Better scout it on foot, hadn't we?"

Silently both men dismounted and tied their horses. Waco slid the Krag from its scabbard, and Jim lifted his own short-barreled, lever-action Winchester from its sheath.

High Rocks. Something of dignity and with a fine sound on the tongue. But the grandmother had stopped that. She had uttered her cackling good-natured laugh and cried out delightedly for Mouse to be reasonable.

"Look at him, boy!" she had challenged, pointing to Heyoka. "Can you put your eyes upon such a noble beast and think of names such as Mighty King or Bear Killer or Great Rock Horse? Observe that lovely head. Study those marvelous limbs. See the trim hoofs. The flashing speed. The splendid grace. *Ai!* Don't miss that grand sweep of mane and tail, either. And the sweet dark eye. And the indescribable beauty of the color of the coat. Ah, there, indeed, is a horse that defies our simple language to describe. *Ih! He-hau!*"

Well, as a matter of truth, the grandmother was right. Mouse had to admit it when he looked at Heyoka, and he had to laugh with the old lady, too. Heyoka was easily worth it.

Peering at the foal now as he continued to frisk about the edges of the pony herd, the boy grinned happily. That was the funniest foal ever dropped by an Oglala mare. Like his mother he had a coat of many colors. But the result in his case was not one of bright spotting. All his hues ran into one another like war paints mixed all in the same dirty clay pot with a muddy stick. He had brilliant blue eyes, also, and the eyes had a staring, odd look to them, and he could make each of them turn in an opposite way at the same time, a disturbing thing to be sure. His rump stood higher by six inches than his shoulder, goose-rumped it was called, and it made him waddle like a duck when he walked away. He was splayfooted as a rabbit in front and cow-hocked as a buffalo calf behind. The grandmother said that he had all four legs fastened on, each in the wrong socket, and Mouse was inclined to agree. He was forever stumbling over himself. If someone tried to sell an Indian a mount like that, the Indian would take it as an

Jim peered down to where the trail came out on a little bench. He could see nothing unusual, but, if Waco had detected motion or something out of place, it was well to stop.

"See?" Waco slid down and joined his partner. "There by the big rock?"

"I don't see a thing," Jim said truthfully.

"Somethin' moved." Waco was past Jim now, and staring toward the bench. "Might have been a rabbit. Might be 'most anythin'. I'll slide on down an' see."

Before Jim could restrain him, Waco was gone, moving down the trail. The bench was not fifteen feet below them.

Emerging from shadow, Waco started across the bench toward the big rock he had indicated, and from the darkness across the cañon a flame bloomed and then came the crash and roar of an explosion, beating back and forth between the cañon walls. Waco was lost to view in the shadow of the rock, and Jim, hearing the high whine of a ricocheting bullet, made the last fifteen feet of the trail to the bench in one, swift, headlong rush. Once again the gun from across the cañon roared, as Jim dived for the shadow of the rock, Winchester across his chest, his thumb on the hammer. As he dropped down into the shelter, he heard Waco cursing.

"Blacker than midnight in a cellar," the little man snarled. "Here we are, right out on the bench an' them in the dark. They caught us just like we was kids in a pantry."

To some extent he was right. The opposite side of the cañon was shadowed, the moon not yet having risen high enough to light it. And, too, Jim and Waco were marooned, but, sheltered by their rock fort, they were in no serious trouble. Moonlight makes uncertain shooting, and a man in shadow cannot pull his front sight down into the notch of the rear with any sureness. Jim grunted and then laughed lightly.

"I cannot tell you," Fox replied. "Iron Road told me to watch the herd for you, and to say no more than I have. I can give you a hint, however. It is all the fault of those old vultures in the Katela lodge."

"The Katela lodge?" repeated Mouse, very frightened now.

This lodge was composed of the widows of warriors fallen in battle. Most of them were squaws with many snows upon their shoulders, and many sons offered in battle to Wakan Tanka, the Great Spirit. But some of them were also the mothers of the young men who had sought out Mato upon the mountain. They were very powerful among the Oglala, those old and young squaws of the Katela lodge. If Iron Road had sent for Mouse on the order of that society, the trouble which the boy had seen running toward him with his friend Fox could be darker than the shadow of Yunke Lo himself.

"Yes, the Katela lodge," Fox answered him solemnly. "You had better hurry now. I'm sorry, Mouse. Good bye."

Mouse looked at the older boy. He drew himself up to stand straight and proud.

"I am not afraid," he said. "Did I fail when I faced Mato up on the mountain?"

"Mato was only a bear. These are old women. *Ai!*"

Mouse looked at him another moment, then nodded sadly.

"That is so, Fox," he said. "Good bye."

Join the Western Book Club and GET 4 FREE* BOOKS NOW!
A $19.96 VALUE!

Yes! I want to subscribe to the Western Book Club.

Please send me my **4 FREE* BOOKS**. I have enclosed $2.00 for shipping/handling. Each month I'll receive the four newest Leisure Western selections to preview for 10 days. If I decide to keep them, I will pay the Special Members Only discounted price of just $3.36 each, a total of $13.44, plus $2.00 shipping/handling ($19.50 US in Canada). This is a **SAVINGS OF AT LEAST $6.00** off the bookstore price. There is no minimum number of books I must buy, and I may cancel the program at any time. In any case, the **4 FREE* BOOKS** are mine to keep.

*In Canada, add $5.00 shipping/handling per order for the first shipment. For all future shipments to Canada, the cost of membership is $16.25 US, which includes shipping and handling. (All payments must be made in US dollars.)

NAME: _____

ADDRESS: _____

CITY: _____ STATE: _____

COUNTRY: _____ ZIP: _____

TELEPHONE: _____

E-MAIL: _____

SIGNATURE: _____

Chapter Seven

The old men of the Council of Elders sat in a half circle before Iron Road's teepee. They smoked their pipes and looked at Mouse as though they were sorry for this thing that they now must do. The boy stood waiting. Iron Road spoke.

"It will be difficult for a young person to understand what has happened," he said to Mouse, "but you must try."

The boy nodded obediently.

"We have taken the vote of the council," the chief continued. "The decision is that the spirit of Mato has entered your body."

Mouse straightened, pleased and proud.

"Do you mean, my chief," he asked, "that I am inhabited by the great brave heart of that king of bears?"

"No, no," admonished Iron Road. "You misunderstood me. It is not his braveness that has stolen into you, but his evilness. We are sad for you, my son."

Mouse was suddenly afraid once more. "What is the matter?" he inquired. "What are you going to do to me?"

"Well," answered Iron Road, "it is not only you, Mouse. Also your grandmother is included. The council has voted that she is guilty, too."

"Guilty of what?" cried the boy. "I have done nothing. My grandmother has done nothing."

"It is not your fault, nor is it hers," said Iron Road.

"Whose fault is it, then, my chief?"

"Mato's fault. Ever since your grandmother released that bear from his cage in our camp, he has hated the Oglalas. Now two more of our people are dead. So the council has ordered that you and your grandmother be banished from the tribe. The spirit of Mato is within you both, and you must leave the camp and stay away from it until Mato is dead."

Mouse could not reply for a moment, then found his voice.

"My chief!" he cried indignantly, "this is not a fair vote. It was many summers ago that my grandmother freed the young bear. How can the council blame her for those two young men who were killed by him only now?"

Iron Road put a gentle hand upon the boy's shoulder. In the chief's dark eyes was compassion. His words were gentle.

"It is the will of the council," he said. "I know it is a harsh vote, yet you must abide by it. It is the law."

"Well," shouted Mouse defiantly, "it is a bad law! When strong men will put out into the wilderness a poor old lady who is crippled and has no wealth of ponies and no men folk to hunt for her, then that is a shameful thing!"

Iron Road accepted the boy's natural anger. But he was bound to do what the council voted, and Mouse knew that.

The council ruled among the Sioux. The boy believed Iron Road was his friend. He did not think the chief agreed with that foolishness about the bear's evil spirit coming to live inside a small lad and his grandmother. Yet there was little that Iron Road might do about it. The mothers of the dead young men, with the other women of the Katela lodge, had gone to the council and told it what must be done.

Mouse shook his head sadly. What a strange thing, he thought. The women sat behind the council circle and did not say a word. They only nodded and smiled and were content. They knew what the vote would be. And why not? Had they not arranged it all along?

But the boy was not bitter. He was only fearful. The old grandmother and he were going to have to go away. They could not travel to some other band, either. The word of their banishment would be spread by the sisters of the Katela lodge. Nowhere among the Sioux would they find a welcome. The sign of evil had been put upon them. From that day they would be like coyotes or buzzards. People would strike at them with sticks. They would be afraid to feed them, or to furnish them with a blanket, or even to give them a kind word. It would be a hard thing, and unjust, yet the boy was an Oglala and had his pride.

"All right, my chief," he told Iron Road, after the latter had excused his anger. "I will go and tell the old grandmother about the vote. How much time are we granted?"

Iron Road pointed upward.

"Until Anpetuwi sleeps," he answered. "Is that fair?"

Anpetuwi was the sun. Glancing at it in his turn, Mouse saw that it stood yet on the morning side of the sky.

"Yes, that is fair," he said. "Thank you." He had turned to depart, when a thought struck him. "Did I understand you to say that the grandmother and I might return to the band when Mato has died?" he asked Iron Road.

"That is so," replied the chief. "When Mato is dead, his spirit will leave the earth. Then it will no longer be in you and your grandmother. Do you see how it is now, boy?"

But Mouse was not entirely satisfied. "I am not sure," he said. "Grizzly bears live many winters. Mato may be alive a long time yet. I may be as old as my grandmother before we may return."

Iron Road shook his head with a grim frown. "I do not believe so," he assured the boy. "The council has voted a war on Mato. It will be to the death . . . his death. You see, Mouse, it is not just the two young men. You have not been told the complete story. Many years ago, when your grandmother let the bear out of the cage, this Mato of yours ran through the camp smashing down both men and women and small children. A child died, and two men, and three women. Since that time, also, he has killed others of the Oglalas. He is an evil spirit and must be destroyed by driving the holy spear through his wicked heart. Our people should have done this long ago, now we will do it."

Mouse thought a moment, then turned to the council, a final hope rising in his mind. "You will pardon me, my fathers," he said politely to the old men. "I understand now why Mato must die. Yet there is another matter that I do not understand. That is concerning my old grandmother. Please, my fathers, do not drive out an old woman because of this evil bear. Let me go, yes. I am young. But she has too many winters, and she has no grown son, nor even a daughter, to help her. She has nothing at all."

When he said that, the oldest man of the council removed his pipe from between his teeth and shook his head. "No, my son," he said, "that is not a true thing you say. Your grandmother has *you*."

Mouse had not expected such respect. He looked back at the old man and at Iron Road and at all the others. Each in his turn nodded his head, agreeing with the ancient one. Mouse felt very proud for a fine moment, then he realized what else was meant by the old man's words.

Suddenly at thirteen summers, he, Tonkalla, the Mouse, was a grown man with a family to look after. In his charge now were a crippled grandmother, her four poor ponies, one old pack mule, and the little wild orphan foal of Rainbow. All that he, Mouse, had with which to perform this new task was a parting gift presented him by Iron Road as he started away from the chief's lodge and the council meeting. This gift was

Old Caniyassa, the flintlock musket that sometimes fired and most times did not.

Other than that it was Mouse against the mountain. Against the mountain and against Mato, the great black grizzly bear.

Chapter Eight

Packing their few belongings, Mouse and his grandmother set forth. A short distance from the camp of Iron Road, the old lady waved to her grandson.

"Let us get down and rest a bit, boy," she suggested. "We must talk and decide which way we are to go in our new lives as outcasts."

"But Grandmother," protested the youth, "we have come only a little way out of sight of the meadow. We do not need to rest yet."

The old squaw looked at him, her wrinkled face crinkling to a hundred smile lines. "Fool boy," she muttered, "I do not want to rest, I want to talk. Don't you know a woman has to talk?"

"I ought to know it, Grandmother." Mouse grinned. "I have lived with you thirteen summers."

"Bah, the young have no respect any more. So now I talk too much, eh? Well, it doesn't matter. My old bones still need to be eased from sitting on this bone pile of a mule."

Mouse looked at Sunsunla, the gaunt pack mule. In Sioux the animal's name meant simply "donkey," but meant it in the sense of one not gifted with great brain power. The grandmother always rode Sunsunla rather than one of their four ponies. She said she did this to punish the old pack mule for his stupidity and stubbornness, but Mouse always felt it was the grandmother who was punished by the ride.

"Donkey," the boy laughed, "do you hear what she is saying about you? Calling you a bone pile? Will you stand there and accept such insults?"

The mule put back his long, moth-eaten ears and brayed with a terrible, unbelievable sound, which stunned the hearing. When he had quite finished, the old lady got down off of him.

"Well," she shrugged, "that is your opinion, Donkey. Now amble along and graze a bit while this new warrior of ours gives his old grandmother some advice. Come, Mouse."

She put her thin arm about the boy's shoulders, and he helped her to a nice, smooth rock beside the trail.

"Grandmother," he said with fierce resentment, "one day I will make those people of ours pay for driving you away!"

"*Ih,*" muttered the old lady, "think no more of them, boy. They were only afraid of us, you see, and, when people know such fear, they will do anything. Forget them."

She sat down on the rock and brought forth her stone pipe. When she had loaded it with tobacco and lighted it, she inhaled the fragrant smoke, nodding thoughtfully. Taking the pipe from her mouth, she pointed with it upward toward the great central mountain, Sotoju.

"No Sioux has been up there," she said, "since the moon in which I freed Mato from his cage. A long time, Mouse."

"Yes," the boy agreed, "a long time, Grandmother."

He said no more, knowing that the old woman would want the next words. Presently she ceased puffing on her pipe, turning her bright, quick eyes upon him.

"Do you think I am crazy in the head as the others say of me, Mouse?" she asked.

"Well,"—the boy smiled—"sometimes you do behave in a strange manner. But I know your brain is good. I think you are trying to fool people. You are like Turtle, my friend who is supposed to be deaf in both of his ears."

"What do you mean, 'supposed to be deaf,' Mouse?"

"Because, Grandmother, Turtle can hear very well when he wishes to."

"And me, boy?"

"Well, you, Grandmother, are only crazy when *you* wish to be."

The old lady threw back her head and cackled like a loon on still water at twilight. Her mouth stretched wide, showing her three remaining teeth to excellent advantage. Mouse thought that, right at that instant, anyone would have believed his grandmother was mad as a rabbit dancing in the moonlight.

"*Ai-eee,*" she sighed at last, wiping the tears of enjoyment from her eyes. "All right, let us say I am crazy only when it suits me . . . which brings us to our problem, however."

"What problem is that?" frowned Mouse.

"Which road we must take from this point, boy."

"Why, that is no problem," he answered. "We must go down the mountain. Down there where it is warmer in the winter and where your bones won't ache so much. You don't suggest that we might go *up,* Grandmother? That we would dare to travel Mato's road which climbs the holy mountain?"

"I don't suggest anything," the old lady replied. "I am only saying that we have a choice of roads. One goes up, and one goes down. Which will it be, Mouse? Careful with your answer, now. I want you to think back to what I taught you about choosing a road, boy."

At that, Mouse brightened. "Oh," he said, "you mean the difference between the hard road and the easy road."

"That's it. Now what about that difference?"

"Well, the hard road runs uphill, the easy road downhill."

"What else?" the old lady insisted.

Mouse frowned again. "I do not like to say it, Grandmother," he answered her.

"Go on, say it," she demanded sharply.

"Well, all right . . . the easy road is for old horses which are weary, or for cowards of all ages who are afraid . . . but the hard road is for warriors who fear nothing."

"That's right," nodded the old lady, satisfied. "Now here we are, Mouse, ready to choose our road." Removing her pipe, she spat accurately at a small rock in the trail. "There is the warm road going down the mountains to the low country, and there is the cold road going up the mountain to Mato's land." She paused, eying her small grandson. "Which road will you take, Mouse?" she said quietly.

The boy could not answer the question. He could not decide what it was the old woman wanted of him. On the point of admitting his weak spirit, he was interrupted by a shout from the trail to the camp. The grandmother and he peered hard through the gathering dusk of the mountain sunset.

Mouse felt his heart beat more quickly. It was his deaf friend, Turtle, running very fast. Turtle *never* ran fast.

Chapter Nine

Turtle was the third of Mouse's three good friends. He moved slowly, talked slowly, and blinked his eyes a lot, but he was not slow of mind.

"Mouse," the boy said when he had panted up, "I have some big news to tell you."

"What is it?" asked Mouse hopefully. "Are we forgiven?"

"Grandmother," Turtle said, ignoring Mouse, "excuse me for not greeting you first. *Woyuonihan.*"

"Sunke waste," laughed the old lady, patting the boy on the head. Mouse would have resented the term, since it meant "good dog," but Turtle only blinked and stuck his neck out farther forward. "Thank you, Grandmother," he said. "I like you."

"Turtle!" warned Mouse, "if you do not tell us the big news, I will whack you with my pony-driving staff!"

Turtle only blinked some more, still ignoring Mouse. "Grandmother," he inquired, "may I borrow your pipe and a little of your tobacco? I came away in such a hurry I forgot to bring my own."

Mouse knew that Turtle did not smoke, but the grandmother graciously handed over the pipe and the pouch. Turtle puffed at the pipe and got it going. Then he began his story.

"As soon as you left the camp," he said, "Iron Road called another council. To the People he said . . . 'Hear me, my children, as you know we have voted a war to the death against Mato, the black grizzly bear. Now I need volunteers of brave heart to go with me and kill Mato. Who will show his hand?' " Turtle blinked at the shameful memory. "Well," he went on, "Iron Road had an easy time counting those hands which showed. Only one went up. That was from our friend, Bald Head. He wanted to be excused."

"What an insult to Oglala pride!" said Mouse. "Then what?"

Turtle started to continue, but the grandmother interrupted him abruptly. "Here," she told him, "give me back my pipe and pouch, Turtle. That's too strong a mixture for boys."

The slow-moving boy nodded in his sober way, obeying her. "To tell the truth, Grandmother," he admitted, "I am glad enough to quit. What do you have in that mixture? I recall asking only for a little tobacco."

"A little tobacco is precisely what you got," barked the old lady. "In addition you received a bit of the red willow dust, some burned millet seed, old sunflower petals, yucca soap weed, and a pinch of dried buffalo chips."

Turtle gulped and turned a greenish shade.

"Go on with your story," ordered the grandmother, not pitying him. "How did Iron Road get those great-hearted warriors of his to go after the bear?"

"He didn't," said Turtle. "He had a better idea."

"Go on, go on!"

"He told them they could get a white man to kill the bear for them. The People shouted that Iron Road had grown soft in the head. What could possibly make a white man want to help an Indian, they demanded to know? *Money,* said Iron Road. And the People cried out, yes, that is so, a white man will do anything for money. But where were they to get the money? By selling all their furs, answered Iron Road. And again the People cried out, yes, yes, but who is the white man that will buy the furs and then hunt the bear instead of paying for the furs in money? In reply, Iron Road made a speech.

"He raised both arms toward the sky. His war bonnet flared into a great burst of feathers, like the sun. His voice rolled like the thunder upon the mountain. 'My people,' he said, 'who has a trading fort but a few pony rides from this camp? Who has married an Indian woman and is a friend to all red men? Who is the most famous hunter and scout in all the Big Rock Mountains, and of either skin color, red or white? *Ai-eee!*' Iron Road's fierce eyes flashed as he saw that his warriors knew which white man he meant. 'Well,' he cried, 'what do you say, my people? Is not Iron Road your chief? Will we go with our furs and ask this white man to help us?'

" *'He-hau, he-hau!'* shouted the warriors bravely. 'Yes, yes, we will do it as you say, our chief . . . we will go at once and ask Big Throat Jim Bridger to kill the great black bear for us . . . !' "

That was the end of Turtle's news. When he had given it, Mouse thanked him and said: "Good bye, old friend, Turtle."

"All right," blinked the other boy in his deliberate way. "Good bye, old friend Mouse."

They made a parting sign to one another, and Turtle started back to the camp. The grandmother wiped a tear from her eye. "There goes a good boy," she said. "Remind yourself to be more like him."

"Very well, I will," agreed Mouse. "But now we had better be going on."

"Of course," said the grandmother, watching him closely. "And which road have you decided to take?"

Mouse frowned uncomfortably. He had hoped to avoid that matter. But now he could see what it was that the grandmother was seeking to find out. It was not the roads, it was Mouse the old lady was interested in.

The boy looked down the lower trail, the easy road. The day's pleasant warmth lingered in that direction. The sun was yet yellow and soft upon the grass of the valley that he could see far below. Then he looked up Mato's road, the hard road. The sun was already behind the mountain up there. The way loomed dark and forbidding. Mouse shivered and almost decided for the warm safe road. But a second thought came strongly to halt him. It had nothing to do with safe and easy or with dangerous and difficult. It was, instead, a matter of what the Sioux called *woco owatanla,* that which is right.

Mato had saved the lives of both Mouse and his grandmother. Now the famous white scout, Big Throat Bridger, was coming to kill Mato. If Mouse went down the mountain, there would be no one to carry the warning to the great bear. If Mouse, however, found the courage to go up the mountain, he might save Mato's life. Which way lay *woco owatanla?* The boy hesitated.

"Grandmother," he said finally, "do you know that Mato is as high in the shoulders as a small pony even on his all fours?"

"Yes," said the old lady, "I know that."

"Do you know also that he stands as tall, almost, as a teepee when he has reared up on his hind legs?"

"Yes, I know that, too, boy."

"And do you know, Grandmother, that his fang teeth are as long as my fingers stretched out as far as I can stretch them?"

"Longer," answered the grandmother without mercy. "They are as long as *my* fingers."

"Well, then," demanded the boy accusingly, "do you still

insist that I have a reasonable choice of roads to make?"

"I do," the old lady replied. "Even more so because of all these things you have said."

It was growing late. Soon they would need to make camp. No Sioux willingly risked being seen by those restless souls of the dead that came out of the ground to roam the night, looking for travelers on the trail after the sun had gone to sleep. Mouse became very nervous.

"Grandmother," he complained, "you are making it hard for me to decide. You should help me more. Remember that I am your grandson."

"That remains to be seen," answered the old lady grimly.

Mouse cast a final look down at the warm sunlight of the meadowland far below. He sent a last glance up at the cold rock of the mountain above. He started to say that his decision was for the easy road, downward to safety. Then he remembered the sound of Mato's soft woofing when the great bear had permitted Mouse and the orphan foal of Rainbow's to live and to go home unharmed. In his memory also he saw again the light of friendship shining in the bear's savage, small eyes. And in that moment of remembering a strange thing happened to Tonkalla, the Mouse.

Of a sudden he felt no fear; he heard his own voice speaking out clearly, with a quiet certainty, to the waiting grandmother, and what he said made the old lady very proud, very happy. "I have decided which road to take," he told her. "I am the grandson of my grandmother. We will take Mato's road. . . ."

Chapter Ten

They went up the dark trail. It was so steep they could not ride but had to walk. Sunsunla, the mule, led the way with the old grandmother clinging to his scrubby tail. Behind her came the four pack horses, Heyoka, and Mouse. The foal grew tired quickly. The boy had to put his shoulder to the little animal's rump and push him up the mountain.

All the while it grew darker and colder. They could not see the sunlight anywhere now. The fear in Mouse became greater. He began to pray out loud to the Great Spirit. The boy had always thought it was a very long distance up to the top of Sotoju where Wakan Tanka dwelled. In consequence, he believed that the louder he prayed, the better chance he might have of being heard. Presently, with the darkness turning blacker and the trail more dangerous, he was shouting to the Great Spirit at the top of his lungs.

Ahead of him the grandmother halted the old mule. "Say there, boy!" she ordered Mouse, "stop that loud praying back there! Come up here where I am. I have something to show you."

Mouse obeyed gladly. When he reached the old woman's side, however, he looked about him and shivered. It was an evil place. A sort of small pocket, or pit, in the towering rocks which formed sheer walls on every side of them. There was light enough only for him to see the grandmother's wrinkled face, and the homely whiskered nose of the mule Sunsunla.

The grandmother pointed ahead.

"See that dark hole in the rock wall up there?" she said.

Mouse peered hard at the rearing blank wall of rock before them. At first, it seemed to him that the trail ended squarely against a great vertical cliff. Then he saw the "dark hole" of which the grandmother spoke.

In ages past, some immense shifting of the mountain had split the cliff asunder. In following centuries the cliff top, decayed by wind and water, had fallen inward to block the upper reaches of the vast crevice, leaving open only its lower portion. It was into the cave-like shadows of this lower opening that the narrow track of Mato's road disappeared.

Shivering again, Mouse turned to the ancient squaw. "I see the place," he said. "What of it?"

"What of it?" echoed the old lady. "Don't you know what it is? That's Mato's den inside there."

The boy thought then that he would smother with fear. But he stood fast. "Grandmother," he said, "don't you think it has grown a little too cold and dark to be joking? We must hurry and find a place to make camp."

"True," she agreed, uttering her cackling laugh. "And this is the place!"

"Grandmother! You can't mean it. Camp with Mato? In his own den? Please, no more of your crazy jokes, now!"

"Boy," she told him sternly, "this is no crazy joke. We are near the end of Mato's road. We must follow it on through this great cliff."

"What? Proceed into this fearsome crevice? Never!"

"Tut, tut. Don't grow so excited. What have I taught you?"

"Many wise things." The youth nodded quickly. "One of which was to be crafty enough to realize when it was time to turn around and run away fast."

"No, no, I mean about being afraid of the dark. Have I not said to you a hundred times that the boy who is frightened by the dark makes the man who is afraid of the day?"

Mouse's frown deepened. He threw back his shoulders. "Stand aside!" he commanded bravely. "I shall enter that chasm of darkness. I shall lead the way into it!"

He started proudly enough into the gloomy crevice, then had another idea.

"On second consideration," he said, halting abruptly, "I believe that I had better return down the mountainside and help little Heyoka to join us. Poor thing, he cannot make such a dangerous climb by himself."

"No!" denied the grandmother sharply. "A time comes when everything must learn to climb the trail by itself. You cannot always be there to help your small horse. You cannot forever be hurrying to guide him up to the steep places he must travel. It is a sorry favor to help weak things too much. It only makes them all the weaker. Pretty soon they are unable to help themselves at all. Leave the foal alone. Let him find his own way up here."

"But Grandmother. . . ."

"*Hookahey,* go ahead!" ordered the old lady, scowling. "Into that dark place with you. Are you a man or a boy?"

"A man!" shouted Mouse, and forced his feet to carry him into the cleft's dismal opening, his heart beating like a rabbit's.

Almost as soon as he was well started into the blackness, however, he saw a luminous glow ahead. The glow grew brighter with each step. Mouse walked faster and faster. He could feel the air in the shadowy cleft becoming warmer as the glow grew brighter still. Then of a sudden the light became dazzlingly brilliant, bathing the narrow passage of the split cliff trail in a shower of golden illumination. The next moment the boy made the final turn in the cleft's winding track and stood gazing out upon a scene that halted his breath with wonder.

He was poised upon a level stretch of granite overlooking an inner valley hidden from the outer world by the towering cliff through which the grandmother and he had followed the secret passageway of Mato's road. The Indian boy released his held breath in a long sigh that spoke far more than any words. It expressed a feeling almost of awe, as though the youth understood that something more mysterious and powerful even than black Mato dwelled here, and that utter silence was the only tribute one might pay to this power.

Everything before him lay bathed in the soft yellow of the day's departing sunlight. All was warm, peaceful, lovely beyond the telling. Mouse could not, he would not speak. His thoughts were overwhelmed by the beauty he saw.

Not so the old grandmother. Behind the boy now, she trudged out of the cliff's inner opening, cheerful as ever.

"Well, this is where we will camp, Mouse," she announced. "This is the end of Mato's road. This is his den, here, this sunlit valley. This is the place to which your decision to follow the difficult way has brought you. How do you like it?"

It was not an easy thing for the boy to answer the question. He had never seen such a wild place, one so entirely lonely yet grandly beautiful. The stillness was so intense it pressed upon the ear. Surely the foot of man had not trod this way for many summers, if ever. The grass grew with only the print of the deer's trim hoof to track its carpet. Only the beaver's home dammed the rush of the fair stream that watered the lush meadow. No slash of axe blade upon the pines, no ugly scars of cook-fire burns upon the ground disfigured the face of Maka, the sacred Mother Earth, in this place.

"What is the valley called?" the boy asked, low-voiced.

"Pangi Anpetuwi," said the grandmother, "Flower of the Sun."

"Sunflower Valley!" murmured Mouse, eyes shining. "What a golden treasure to come upon after such a dark and fearsome trail. And you knew of it, all the time, Grandmother?"

"Ai," said the old lady. "Remember that. I brought you here to teach you the lesson of trust. Also to let you teach yourself some other lessons. You and Mato and that small clown of a foal that comes now behind you. *Ih!* good luck to all of you."

The same moment she finished speaking, Mouse heard behind him the happy whickering of Heyoka. He turned about delightedly. There was little Clown standing weak and wobbly-kneed but proud of himself for having climbed the dark mountain without help.

"Come and see our new home," Mouse greeted him. "Isn't it lovely?"

Clown grunted and stretched out his thin neck. He sniffed the sunset breeze coming to them gently over the meadowland. He snorted and kicked up his heels and ran out into the grass and fell down and rolled over and over in it after the manner of a young dog released from a teepee staking chain. That was his answer, his way of telling his master how he liked Sunflower Valley.

The old pack horses coming out of the passageway a moment later also pricked up their ears and whinnied their delight to greet the wondrous smells of mountain grass and singing-clear mountain water. Even Sunsunla, the obstinate and moth-eaten mule, was pleased. He announced his opinion with one of his terrible brays, a sound to awaken the dead.

Covering her ears at the frightful noise, the grandmother seized Mouse's pony-driving stick away from the boy. With a great *whhaackkk!* she laid it across the haunches of Sunsunla.

"Here, you fool Donkey!" she shouted. "Don't you know a holy place when I have brought you to one? Stop that bellowing this instant. You want Wakan Tanka to drive us back out of here before we even settle down?"

Mouse laughed heartily to see the old mule tuck in his ragged tail and run like a colt to escape the grandmother's lusty aim with the pony-driving stick. But the old lady wheeled at once upon him and to his complete astonishment fetched the boy a solid blow with the stick in the same place she had used it upon Sunsunla.

"You, too, loafer!" she cried. "Do you think I guided you all the way up here to stand and cackle as though your empty head had nothing in it to stop the summer winds from blowing in your one ear and out the other? Hah! Go gather some firewood. Trot down to the stream and fetch me a bucket of cooking water. Catch up that old white mare with the food bags tied on her. *Hopo, hookahey!* You're no more use than a stuffed chipmunk!"

The boy felt at home then. All was well in the little family of Ousta, the Limper. He ducked the old lady's stick and ran down into the meadow. She threw an oath after him, and the stick with it. He picked up the stick and gave the white mare a whack with it. She kicked him in the shin and nearly broke his leg bone for the attention. Badly as the kick hurt, Mouse had to laugh once more and to fling wide his arms with good feeling.

"*Hohahe!*" he called thankfully aloud. "Welcome everyone to our new home in Sunflower Valley!"

Chapter Eleven

The next morning Mouse did not awaken until the sun was high. Careful not to disturb the snoring of the grandmother, he got up and pulled apart the ashes of last night's fire. A spiral of smoke arose. He saw three red sparks glowing among the ashes. Bending, he blew upon the sparks, at the same time taking some dried moss and sprinkling it upon them. The smoke puffed more thickly, and a tiny flame spurted from it. Adding a few twigs and then some larger wood, the boy soon had a cheerful breakfast fire crackling.

"Wake up now, Grandmother!" he called. "I am going to cook you some of that buffalo meat you stole from Iron Road's teepee. You know that piece? The one you took while the chief was telling me to leave the camp and take you with me?"

The old lady sat bolt upright upon her blanket. "Certainly I remember the piece!" she cried indignantly. "But it was borrowed, not stolen! I thought as long as it was Iron Road's idea to drive us away, he might as well be the one to loan us a small piece of meat until we might pay him back."

"A small piece?" said the boy curiously. "Grandmother, I don't see how you carried it off without breaking your poor bones. It was a half of a young buffalo nearly."

The old lady frowned, looking away from Mouse. "Well, it was dark inside Iron Road's teepee. I couldn't see what I was doing very well. I thought it was a small piece."

"Grandmother," the boy said, laughing, "I am glad you are not against me. I would rather fight Mato than you. The great bear is forthright, at least. You have no conscience at all."

"A fine way to talk to your only grandmother," grumped the old lady. "Keep blowing on that puny fire instead of puffing at me. I want to smell that fat meat sizzling on the broiling sticks when I get back from the stream."

She set off across the meadow singing a cheerful morning song to herself and to the birds that joined her on the way. She was going to take her bath, Mouse knew. She was of the old Sioux ways, thinking it a sin not to cleanse the body at least once each day, winter and summer. The boy had never known his grandmother to go dirty in all her days. Ragged, yes. Poor, indeed. And wrinkled and careless and cracked in the head perhaps. But unclean? Never. Such a thing was *wicowicasa sni* to the true Oglala; it was wrong.

When the old lady came back to the fire from her plunge into the icy waters of the creek, she stopped in her tracks.

"*Ai!*" she cried, sniffing the smoky air. "Just smell that buffalo meat broiling! Is it not wonderful, Mouse? Now if we had only some of the white man's *pejuta sapa* and a little of his *can hanpi,* we could feast like chiefs!" She sighed regretfully. "Ah, well, too much happiness is bad for the liver. Pass me my piece of the meat, boy."

Mouse held up his hand, requesting her to wait a moment. Then he pointed to the iron pot of water he had placed on the forked sticks over the fire.

"I am still the grandson of my grandmother." He grinned. "Take a good look and a good smell when I lift this lid."

"*Ai-eee!*" yelled the old lady, when he had done so. "It is *pejuta sapa!*"

"Of course, it is coffee," Mouse agreed. "But that is not all. I have some *can hanpi,* too."

"No! Some white man's sugar? Impossible."

She fell to her knees beside the fire, reaching to pour herself a cup of the wonderful white man's coffee. Then she stopped, an expression of the pure in spirit crossing her face.

"Wait!" she cried. "Where did you get it? I won't touch it if you stole it."

"Stole it, Grandmother?" Mouse inquired innocently. "You would believe that I, your own grandson, stole coffee and sugar like some miserable Comanche or Pawnee?"

"No," said the old lady. "More like some miserable Sioux. Like some miserable Oglala Sioux, to be precise. One of about thirteen summers from the band of Iron Road."

"Grandmother! What a thing to say."

"Ah, that is so, a thousand pardons, Mouse. From whom did you borrow the coffee and sugar?"

"From Elkbones, that old rascal who pointed his pipe at me in the council and told me I was a man. He had just been to Big Throat's trading fort. There was this big bag of coffee beans and this other big bag of sugar still on his brown mare tethered by his teepee. I just changed bags to our old white mare. Everything was honest."

The grandmother glared at him searchingly. "Of course, you left Elkbones something of equal value in exchange," she said.

"Of course."

"What did you leave?"

"Why, my perfectly good red moccasins."

"Do you mean the ones with the bottoms worn out of them and too small for you three summers ago?"

"Those are the ones, Grandmother. I hated to part with them, but one must surrender something dear for such a large amount of coffee and sugar."

"Yes, that is true." The old lady nodded, grinning. "You

are a good boy, Mouse. You might have been dishonest and left Elkbones something like a prime fox pelt or a fine curly buffalo robe. But you were very generous, instead."

The boy blushed modestly. "Thank you, Grandmother," he murmured. "But, after all, I am your own true grandson. Could I have done less?"

"True, true indeed," chortled the old lady. "What a blessing we are to one another!"

She threw back her head and burst out with her delighted loon's cackle. Mouse joined her in the wild laughter.

They poured their cups of the hot black coffee, putting in it great pinches of precious white sugar. Between crispy bites of the brown and crackling buffalo meat, they drank the sweet, steaming brew and sang together an Oglala prayer song of greeting to the morning sun.

> *Anpetuwi woyuonihan wakan zizi*
> **Old yellow god of the new day,**
> **We salute you.**
> **Welcome back from the darkness.**
> **Your children always miss you.**
> **They always love you.**
> **They always hope you stayed**
> **Safe and warm**
> **On your long journey. . . .**

Chapter Twelve

The breakfast finished, Mouse repacked the white mare and the other ponies. Then he caught the mule, Sunsunla, for the grandmother to ride, and the rickety brown gelding Quick Horse for himself. Helping the old lady up on her mount, he smiled at her and climbed on the gelding.

"Well, Grandmother," he said, "which way shall we set out around the valley to find our new home?"

"Now that's a serious matter," answered the old lady. "We must be most cautious about it."

She held out her left hand, the palm upward. Spitting into the palm, she slapped it with her other hand. The spittle flew outward to land in the dust toward the right.

"That's the way to go," she said. *"Hookahey!"*

It was a lovely trip. The morning passed very quickly. Almost before Mouse knew it, the sun was standing overhead and it was time for the noon halting. The grandmother stopped by a small creek that tumbled out of the mountain wall at a swift pace to join the larger stream out in the valley.

"We will rest here a little," she said. "My old bones are telling me this is a good place to stop."

"All right," nodded Mouse, although he wanted to go on.

"Waste." The old lady smiled. "You're a good boy, Mouse. Run along and explore up this small stream while I sit here and listen to the water sing."

"There is nothing around here that I want to see," said

Mouse. "It is very plain and rocky."

The old lady looked at him slyly out of one eye. "Well, now, you never know, boy. It's the plain places that deceive. Why not look farther up the stream? Say up there where those two granite rocks make a gateway? My old bones tell me you ought to go up there. I can hear a waterfall, I think. It's probably between those two rocks."

Mouse agreed to go, with a scowl. She had defeated him once more. How could one win an argument with her old bones?

Still grumbling to himself, he struggled up the steepening creekbank. Soon he stood at the foot of the two granite boulders, and the old lady had been right again. There was a waterfall tumbling between the gateway rocks as high as a sixteen-pole Cheyenne lodge.

The boy looked upward, thinking he could go no farther. Then he saw that the trail continued up through the other granite outcrops that flanked the falls. From even a few paces down the small stream one could not see the trail. Even standing as Mouse was, staring right at the rocks, it was difficult to make out the narrow track. How the grandmother had been able to believe from far off that *something* lay up this way was only one more tribute to the old lady's remarkable powers. Mouse nodded to himself. It was not her old bones that gave her this ability, he told himself, it was her old brains. And they were most remarkable, indeed.

Quickly he scrambled up the rocky zigzag path of the trail beside the waterfall, lured as are all boys by the excitement of what might wait just out of sight. Presently he reached the top of the path and could see what lay beyond the waterfall's cascading tumble over the granite ledge. *There before him was the place.*

Level, it was, and covered to the height of a young lad's

knee with thick grasses so deep in color as to seem almost blue rather than green. The grasses were flecked like sunny waters with white daisies, purple morning glories, and pink Indian lilies. Here and there over this meadow carpet stood sentinel pine trees, great lordly giants that had grown since Wakan Tanka made the earth. At the borders of the meadow smaller cedars, firs, spruce, and balsams sheltered the mountain's surrounding slopes.

At the rear of the hidden meadowland before him, the clear waters of the creek widened into a tiny lake. Deep lavender in its center, it was lit with yellow sunlight along its shallows. From far above it, falling from a height so lofty Mouse could not see it from the meadow floor, the creek plunged downward into the tiny lake in a wild feathery heap of lacy waters. A thousand times a thousand rainbows glinted through the vapors of this fall, and it was while peering in wonderment at these *wikmunkes* dancing over the lake that Mouse beheld the final, strangest sight of all. *It was a white man's house of logs!*

The mossy cabin was built so skillfully among the rocks and pines of the lakeshore that none but an Indian eye would have seen it. Mouse shook his head, blinked his eyes, shaded his vision for one more look. The log house was still there. No smoke issued from its chimney. No sign of human movement came from it. Nor was there any sound made by man about it.

"*Hi-ye-he,*" murmured Mouse aloud, and turned and ran all the way back down to where the grandmother was napping with the horses.

Rushing up to the drowsing old lady, he could barely speak. "Grandmother," he finally managed, between gasps, "you will never imagine what I have found up there! It is a white man's little, log house! Your old bones were right about that place, the waterfall and everything. There is even a lavender lake with a second waterfall so high it comes out of the sky, I think. *Wowicake!* You will not believe it!"

In view of her grandson's great excitement the old lady seemed remarkably calm. Perhaps it was the noonday quiet. "Is that so, boy?" She yawned. "Well, now, isn't it peculiar what old bones can foretell?"

"Grandmother," Mouse pleaded, "do not tease. Come and see for yourself. Leave the horses. Hurry!"

"Very well," sighed the old lady. "I'll go. But there's no use leaving the horses. We'll only have to come back for them."

"But the path is too narrow for them, Grandmother."

"Bring the horses, as I say," insisted the old lady. "Perhaps you are right, but let us do it my way this once. Just to be fair to my old bones, eh?"

Mouse quickly agreed. After all, she was a very old lady. She was wrong, of course, but it would not harm Mouse to be generous with her. His good heart was wasted, however. The horses climbed up the steep path beside the waterfall as if it were a level prairie road to the buffalo pastures. By the time all of them had reached the top of the falls and come out into the upper meadow, Mouse was eying the old lady with a great deal of doubt.

"Grandmother," he demanded of her sternly, "are you certain it was your old bones which told you of this place?"

She looked at him with a child's simple stare. "Mouse," she observed, "nothing is certain, not even my old bones. Come on, *hopo,* let's go see that log house."

She scrambled up on Sunsunla once more, lively as a cricket, and gave him a great kick in the ribs. The old mule set off across the meadow, running like a yearling colt. Mouse called to Clown to follow along, then whacked his own brown gelding with the heels of his moccasins.

The bony gelding snorted and lunged forward. Mouse nearly fell off. He ran lightly as the deer. Little Heyoka, Clown, was left far behind. The grandmother cackled wildly as a flying prairie chicken and kicked her ancient mule again. Mouse yelled happily and did the same for Quick Horse. And that is the way in which they all came to their new home in the secret tiny meadow high on the side of Pangi Anpetuwi, the Valley of the Sunflowers.

Chapter Thirteen

Mouse had never seen a white man's house at close range. He had not even been inside a trading fort such as Big Throat's. Now, as the grandmother and he went toward the log cabin, the boy's heart beat hard against his ribs.

"Do not be afraid," counseled the old lady. "No one is here."

She strode to the house and rapped her knuckles on the front of it.

"This is called the door," she instructed the fearful Mouse. "It is where you go in. Watch." She gave the door a kick, and it flew open, leaving a tall hole in the wall of logs to walk through. Mouse was amazed. Yet more was to come. When they had gone inside, the grandmother gave the door a second kick, and it flew back the opposite way, closing the hole in the logs faster than the blinking of a firefly's light.

"*Hmunha!*" cried Mouse. "Run, Grandmother!"

"Be quiet," the old lady said. "Stop that yelling. It is only the way the door works. You open it with a kick, you close it with a kick. But it never falls down. It just goes back and forth forever."

"Wonderful," breathed Mouse.

"*Shhh!*" ordered the grandmother. "We are disturbing the small folk who live here."

It was dark as a cave in the cabin. Mouse could see nothing. He could hear nothing.

"Hello, little ones," called the old lady. "We have come to share your home with you. Do not be alarmed. Now I am going to open the window. We need some light in here."

Mouse heard her move across the floor, then a burst of sunlight came out of the wall of the cabin, dazzling him.

"This is a window," the grandmother explained to the astonished youth. "It's a small door cut out high up in the wall. It lets in light and fresh air yet keeps out rain and cold snow."

"Wonderful," Mouse said again.

Turning from the window, he examined the cabin's interior by its flooding light. There was an eating table and two benches in the middle of the room. Beyond were one chair to sit in and a wooden bed of poles. Mouse had seen such things among the belongings of white men moving across his country in the great canvas-covered wagons of the Oregon Trail. So he was not surprised by them. Moreover, his attention was immediately drawn to the occupants of the eating-table top. These were the grandmother's "small folk" who lived in the cabin: two brown elf owls, a fat field mouse, three scrawny pack rats.

"Mouse," said the grandmother, "open the door for me." She picked up a ragged old bear-grass broom, standing in one corner of the room, and addressed herself further to the chief pack rat. "Pack Rat," she informed him, "right now our new house needs a sweeping out. You and the other little ones must go outside and wait until I am through. Then you are welcome to return, of course, for it is your house, also."

The pack rat, an old graybeard of a fellow with a villainous and crafty eye, chattered to his two companions. They, in turn, consulted the owls and the field mouse. Then the chief pack rat bristled his tail at the grandmother and gave her an indignant squeak of denial.

"Very well," sighed the old lady, tightening her grip on the bear-grass broom. "It would have been nicer my peaceful way." She raised the broom. "Get out now, scat! you miserable ragged loafers, you!"

With this, she swatted at the small beasts with the broom, beating the table top with it as though it were a war drum. The pack rats leaped for their lives. The field mouse dove down through a knothole in the table's planks. The owls flew out through the window and away. A great cloud of ancient dust arose from the grandmother's continuing swings and whackings with the broom. Mouse, too, retreated through the doorway, coughing and sneezing. In a moment, though, the old lady appeared out of the settling dust billows to join him.

"There," she said triumphantly, "that's done. I always dislike cleaning work. It takes so much time. Where did those ungrateful scoundrels go who used to live in there with us, Mouse? What gratitude they showed. *Ih!*"

The boy shook his head in bewilderment. "Grandmother, I will never understand you," he said. "One moment you are telling the poor things to be at ease, the next moment you are trying to swat them with the broom."

"What?" cried the old lady. "Didn't you hear what that rascally pack rat called me?"

"Grandmother, are you saying you understand pack-rat talk?"

"Of course, I do."

"And you mean to have me believe the old gray-beard pack rat insulted you?"

"He certainly did."

Mouse shook his head once more, surrendering. "Grandmother," he sighed, "you're crazy."

"That is exactly what the pack rat said," huffed the old lady. "Come on, boy, follow me. Our new home is ready."

It was a wonderful small house of logs, as Mouse had observed. Low and snug to the ground, a tall man could not have stood erect inside it. Yet for Mouse and the grandmother, both small people, it was perfect. The old lady seemed also to know a considerable number of things about the little dwelling, once her grandson had "discovered" it by following the faint trail past the first waterfall in obedience to the instructions from her old bones.

The cabin had been built many snows before, she told him, more snows ago than the number that had fallen since his own birth. The man who had built it had been a white man—a trapper of the beaver, one of those strange and lonely early-day fur hunters of his people who had come into the Indian lands long, long before the settlers and the gold-seekers who now threatened to overrun the buffalo pastures and to drive out the red man, or to cheat him in trade and deceive him by treaty, and so ruin him without war. In those earlier days the white man and the Indian had been friends, and this white man who built the marvelous small house of logs had been a good friend to the Oglalas. He had even been a special friend of Ousta herself, but that had been long ago, and she had been a young woman and very pretty then.

The old lady sighed with her memories at this point, and Mouse quickly patted her hand. He could not imagine that she was telling the truth. Had he not known her all his life? And had she not always been old and wrinkled? Of course. But he was a good boy, kind and considerate, so he smiled and patted her thin hand once more, and told her how beautiful he was certain that she had formerly been.

Moreover, it was the house that caught at the imagination of the Sioux youth, and not the story of the fur trapper who had built it in the days when Ousta, the Limper, did not limp.

The roof of the tiny structure was of lodgepole pine trunks

trimmed straight as lance hafts. Upon the outer surface of this roof the white trapper had piled much dirt, then cut meadow sods and implanted them atop the rich earth. The sods had rooted and grown until they covered the entire roof, making it appear as a natural part of the meadow itself. The deep sod kept the cabin cool in summer, warm as banked coals in winter, and it never leaked a drip or drop of rainwater in any season.

There was, however, one minor trouble with it. The grass that grew upon it was of such fine quality that their ponies cast greedy eyes toward it. It was Sunsunla that caused the greatest difficulty. The ponies could be driven away and would stay away. Sunsunla was not so simple. The mule would wait quietly until long after dark, then sneak up on the roof top and commence grazing by the midnight stars. On many a middle of the night the grandmother would sit bolt upright in her bed.

"Mouse!" she would yelp in a piercing screech. "There comes another clod of dirt in my eye. That fool Donkey is on the roof again. Get up and drive him away!"

Then Mouse would have to crawl out of his own warm blankets to go and find his pony-driving stick, clamber up on the grass roof, and whack Sunsunla across his stubborn rump. With that, the mule would run off, braying and kicking, and, of course, knocking still more dirt in the old lady's eyes while, at the same time, managing to step on or kick the boy so that Mouse's howls would be added to the mule's hee-hawing and the grandmother's yammerings from below. But it was still a remarkable roof—especially, Mouse felt, in the summertime, such as when he and the grandmother came there. Then it was all pink and white with Indian lilies and mountain daisies and smelled beautifully all of the night long—even with a mule on it.

Their life the first two moons in the little house was as kind as a dream. The weather was good and so was the hunting. The grandmother cooked and kept the house clean; Mouse supplied the small game for the boiling pot or the broiling stick. The two brown owls and the field mouse never returned, but the three rascally pack rats came back every night to renew their war with the grandmother. Between them and the mule on the roof Mouse missed quite a bit of sleep, but he had to admit that he enjoyed the old lady's battle with the "three thieves," as she called them. It was an experience to bring a bow of respect from any boy for his old grandmother. The old lady knew words in the Oglala tongue that Mouse had never imagined. That early summer he acquired a supply of Sioux oaths that made him certain he could swear more admirably than any other Indian boy in tribal memory, and he owed it all to gentle little Ousta, the Limper. Such a grandmother was a true gift.

So the summer passed for them in the little log house of the white man. Birds sang, bees hummed, soft winds whispered during the days. Pack rats squealed, a mule brayed, an old lady cursed during the nights. It was a lovely summer.

But a chill in the air was coming. Mouse first felt it on the final day of the August Moon, their third month in Sunflower Valley. He was never to forget the evil moment.

Chapter Fourteen

Mouse had spent the early summer studying the great grizzly bears that roamed the main valley below. He had come to know most of them. There was Mato Wakanto, High Bear, tall and thin. There was Mato Wasi, White Bear, coat faded to the color of dirty snow, and Mato Hopa, Pretty Bear, a lovely female of exquisite fur and form. Then there was Ikuhansuka, old Long Chin, Wacipi, the Dancer, Wa Klure, the Loafer, and many more, but mostly there was Mato Sapa, Mouse's bear, the black one. Perhaps that was because the boy did not see him so often as the others. He was more aloof, staying much alone, seeming to have no family and no certain home place in the valley. He was more like a great dark shadow than a bear of flesh and bone.

Mouse watched him secretly and by the countless hours. He saw him take his bath, dust himself, let the sun warm his belly. He saw him fish in the stream, hunt mice in the meadow, dig grubs out of old rotten logs, scoop beetles from beneath overturned rocks. There was no magic, either, in this miracle of secret spying. But there was a story to it.

One morning early after their arrival the grandmother called the boy outside the log house at sunrise. She had one hand behind her back, holding onto something which she did not want Mouse to see.

"Boy," she said, "I am going to show you my gratitude for your brave heart in coming so far with me to Sunflower

Valley, and I am nothing but a poor and helpless old lady."

Hearing this, Mouse began to back away from her cautiously. Knowing this "poor and helpless old lady" as he did, he suspected something less than gratitude was about to be shown to him. He well recalled just such a time long ago. Then the grandmother had asked him to hold out his own hand and cover his eyes with the other hand—she was going to give him a nice surprise. Well, she had all right. It had been a piece of juicy antelope tallow with red pepper buried inside it. When Mouse had popped it into his mouth, it felt as though he had swallowed a small fire. Yet he had to admit that the old lady had taught him the lesson she wanted to— for him not to believe everything he was told, not to obey orders without thinking, not to grow careless with people who offered gifts for no good reason. But now, even though he remembered the long-ago experience, he decided he did not want to hurt the grandmother's feelings by showing suspicion.

"Very well," he told her, "go ahead. I am ready."

"Good," she said. "Hold out your one hand."

"Grandmother," he warned, "if you are now going to add, 'cover your eyes with the other hand,' I am not going to do it."

"Ah!" she cried, very pleased. "I see that you have not forgotten the antelope fat and red pepper. But don't worry about any tricks this time. We are both older now."

Mouse closed his eyes so as not to spoil her surprise, then held his hand out. He felt an object being placed in the hand. He did not recognize the feel of it.

"*Onhey!*" said the grandmother, using the word for the old Sioux way of giving a present to be kept always.

The boy opened his eyes, and those eyes grew misty then. The grandmother had given him her most precious treasure:

a brass "long eye," a telescope given to her many years ago by some Pony Soldiers of the white people for her service in guiding them safely through the dangerous country of the Crow Indians.

There was nothing Mouse could say to show the old lady his true gratitude. But ah! there was much that he could do with that marvelous brass telescope to demonstrate for her his pleasure in the gift and her wisdom in the giving.

It was from that morning of her generosity that he grew into the habit of watching the great bears move about the valley below, accomplishing this in safety through the eye of the telescope and from the comfort of the granite ledge above the lower waterfall. And it was in the practice of this habit that he came to be upon the ledge the final morning in the Moon of August, the morning when the chill wind first blew into the high Valley of the Sunflowers.

Mouse did not know why it was, but the moment he lay down upon the granite ledge with the telescope he knew something was wrong. Even without the "long eye" of the glass he could see that the valley was empty, strangely quiet. It came to him that even the meadowlarks were not singing. He raised the telescope and swept the valley with it end to end. He saw nothing whatever of movement.

He lowered the telescope, for some reason much afraid. He thought at first to run and ask the grandmother to come and look at the valley. Then he heard the far warning cry of an eagle, wheeling in the sky. Marking the bird's position, he felt another twinge of the strange foreboding. The eagle was circling above the place where the dark chasm brought Mato's trail through the great cliff into Sunflower Valley.

Mouse raised the telescope again. Focusing it, he aimed its lens toward the far distant exit of the trail. *Be calm,* he counseled himself. *It must be only Big Throat Bridger come to* hunt Mato. *Big Throat is a friend to our people. He will not harm us. He has come to do what the Oglalas paid him the money from their many furs to do . . . to hunt down the great black bear and remove his evil spirit from the band of Iron Road.* Then Mouse brightened. *There is even more,* he told himself soberly, yet with growing delight. *Big Throat is here to remove the spirit of Mato from the grandmother and from myself, as well. We will be able to go back down the mountain and live with our people once again.* Waste! *That is good!*

But even as he cheered himself, the Oglala boy continued turning the eyepiece of the telescope to bring its image more sharply into focus at the mouth of Mato's chasm far up the valley. It was then that the chill wind struck him, when, through the telescope, he saw the man who was standing at the cliff trail's exit *inside* the valley. That man was not Big Throat Jim Bridger.

He was another white man. A tall, black-bearded, evil man with a face like the blade of a killing axe, and only one good eye in that face. It was that one eye which chilled the Indian youth. It was staring right back at him through a telescope just like his own!

Mouse ran toward the log house. The grandmother herself at that same moment came out of the cabin doorway on the run. But she had not seen Mouse's approach. She had Old Caniyassa, the pony herd rifle, in her hands. She was waving the weapon and sending out curses like bullets.

"Thief! Robber! Rascal! This time you have gone too far. Steal my piece of breakfast meat, will you? Hah!"

She raised the rifle, still running, and then Mouse saw scooting along the ground ahead of her the skinny chief of the pack rats. The pack rat was struggling with a piece of meat far too big for him to carry. Between this burden and his need to watch backward for the grandmother and the rifle, he did not see Mouse in time. He ran squarely between the boy's feet. As he did, the latter reached down and caught him by the tail.

"Good boy, good boy!" shrieked the old lady, dashing up. "Now hold him tightly so that I may put the muzzle of this musket right between his beady eyes!"

"No, don't shoot!" pleaded Mouse. "That old rifle is loaded to the muzzle nearly. That's a full bear load that I have crammed in there. It will blast away everything around this shabby little rat, including your only grandson."

"Get out of my way, then," ordered the grandmother. "I am going to shoot. Throw him down, Mouse, and stand back!"

Instead of throwing the pack rat to the ground, the boy whirled him about his head and threw him far out into the lake, where he alit with a flat splash.

"Keep running when you land on the far shore," Mouse called after him. "When the Limper has her shooting eye on fire, nothing smaller than a bear is safe!"

The next thing was to get the musket away from the grandmother. This Mouse tried to do by explaining that the load in the rifle was their *only* load. It had to be saved should they meet Mato on the trail and the great bear not yield the path to them. Even so the old lady would not be persuaded until the boy held out the piece of meat he had rescued from the pack rat.

"Here," he said. "I will trade you this fine piece of breakfast meat for the old rifle. What do you say?"

At that, she smiled and nodded happily. "Why, bless you, boy." She cackled. "I was just going to have a bit of meat for breakfast, isn't that strange?"

Mouse gave her the meat and took the musket.

"Listen," he said quickly. "We have no time for breakfast really. There is an evil-looking white man coming down the valley. I saw him come out of Mato's road through the mountain. I saw his face in the telescope as big as my own face. And he saw me likewise in the same manner."

When he said the white man had seen him in return, the grandmother seized him by the shoulders excitedly. "Are you certain that he saw you, too?" she croaked. "How could you be sure at such a great distance?"

"A very simple way to tell," Mouse answered. "He had a telescope, also, and he was looking at me at the same time I was looking at him."

"Ai-eee!" groaned the old lady. "That is very bad."

"That's what I thought. It is why I came running so quickly to tell you. What must we do?"

The grandmother studied him a moment. She put her head to one side in the way she used when something not-so-crazy was forming in her crafty mind. Then she nodded swiftly.

"It is not what we will do that is the question," she said to Mouse. "It is what he will do." She paused a long second or two, then added: "Come on, boy, we must get ready for him."

"*Ready* for him, Grandmother?" Mouse asked in a small uncertain voice. "In what way?"

"In the very best way," she answered, "that two poor Indians can get ready to meet an unknown white man. Come, we must hurry . . . !"

Chapter Fifteen

Mouse crouched behind the windowsill in the log house, watching the white man ride across the meadow on his rat-tailed gray horse. The old lady sat outside the cabin beside the breakfast fire. She was singing one of her peculiar prayer songs. To look at her one would not imagine she had a care in the world, or that she knew anyone else was within a dozen pony rides of the sound of her voice. Mouse felt his nerves tightening.

Over in the tall grass by the lake their ponies grazed contentedly, Heyoka, the clown-like foal, among them. The wind being away from them, the animals did not scent the approach of the strange horse. Mouse had wanted to hide Heyoka and the others back in the pine trees, but the grandmother had thought otherwise.

"This white man knows we have horses," she had said. "I believe that is why he comes seeking us, because of our spare horses."

When Mouse had inquired how it was she believed this, the old lady had frowned quickly. "You told me he had but one horse of his own, the one he is riding. From that I understand he would require at least another horse, perhaps more."

"Another horse, or more? For what, Grandmother?"

"For the business which I am guessing has brought him up here in this high valley of Mato's. Now go and get in the house and hide yourself beneath the window as I have told you. Remember, all depends on you."

This had been but minutes before. Now the white man drew near, guiding his mount up the creek-side trail toward them. As he came up, the grandmother did not look his way, but commenced to sing her aimless song louder than ever.

> *Co-o-o, co-o-o*, it is daybreak
> In the village.
> *Owanyeke waste*, everything is
> Good to the eye.
> *Wowa un sila*, my heart is full
> Of sympathy for all.
> *Hunhanni hopa*, what a beautiful
> Morning it is.
> *Wowicake he iyotan wowa sake*,
> Truth is power.
> *Wasna chashasha skuya*,
> I have meat, tobacco, and salt.
> *Hunhunhe, hunhunhe*,
> I am happy!

The white man halted his horse across the fire from the ancient Oglala squaw. He touched the fingers of his left hand to his forehead in the Sioux gesture of respect.

"*Woyuoihan*," he said, speaking the Oglala tongue perfectly. "*Kola tahunsa*, I am your friend, your cousin. I come in peace."

He smiled when he spoke, and over beneath the window-sill Mouse shivered with fear.

But the grandmother was not afraid. "*Hohahe*, welcome," she said. "You have the grin of a panther smelling fawn meat. What do you want?"

The man rubbed the dirty patch that covered his bad eye.

The other eye glared at the old squaw. Then the twisted smile appeared once more. The man got down from his horse, his long Kentucky rifle in his hand.

"Why, granny," he said, "don't you remember me?"

"I don't see how I could forget you," answered the old lady, "but I have done so."

The man rested the butt stock of the rifle on the ground. "Now that's a pity, granny. I am not flattered. I remember you. You're old Ousta, the Limper, out of Iron Road's band."

"You speak Oglala as though you were born on a buffalo robe." The grandmother nodded, squinting across the smoke of the fire.

"You're not far off," leered the man, rolling his one eye about in its socket. "I've slept on enough buffalo robes to be a chief ten times over. Hee hee hee!"

He had a silly, high-pitched laugh. It was like that of a person not right in his mind. Yet he could cut the laugh off and replace it with the dog snarl twisting of his lips—as he did then—in the time it required to blink his single eye. Watching him, Mouse became so frightened of him that he had to clench his teeth tightly to prevent their rattling so loud the man might hear them. Still, the old grandmother showed no more fear of their black-bearded guest than she did of any man, which was no fear at all.

"Well, now, white cousin, let us have the truth," she said. "You know my name, so tell me yours." As the man hesitated, scowling at her, she shrugged slyly. "Come, what is there to fear from a poor old lady all alone in the mountains?"

"All alone?" challenged the man instantly. "What about the boy? Where is he? Don't lie to me, old woman. I saw him through my telescope."

"Why should I lie, white cousin? I sent the boy away to hide until you had gone. He doesn't like white men."

"Oh? And how about you, old lady?"

The grandmother threw back her head, releasing her wild laugh, startling her questioner into a curse. "Me?" she said. "Why, everyone knows that we Oglalas love the white man. Hee hee!"

"For a fact everyone does," nodded the man. "There isn't a Sioux tribe on the plains with a worse reputation for hating the whites. You Oglalas are natural born killers."

"Very true," admitted the grandmother. She pursed her lips as if to some distasteful taint. "Would you mind moving yourself?" she inquired politely. "The wind has changed so that it blows to me from your direction. *Phew!*"

The white man's face darkened with rage. "Why you sneaking old she-dog, you!" he snarled. He raised the long rifle, cocking its hammer with a loud click. "For that I will blow a hole through your belly."

"You stink like a wet dog in a warm teepee," said the old lady. "Go ahead, shoot."

Mouse, thinking the end had come for the grandmother, was at the point of leaping through the window and racing to her aid when, of a sudden, she raised her hand.

"No, wait," she said to the white man. "First tell me why you come here. What is it you want? Surely you can satisfy an old lady's curiosity before shooting her."

"You know what I came here for, granny. And you know what I want from you. I want your horses."

"All of them?"

"I would have taken just one. But now I will take them all, and kill you into the bargain. Does that satisfy your curiosity, old lady?"

"One other thing, white cousin," the grandmother requested quickly, holding up her hand once more for him to wait. "Tell me your name. You know it is bad manners to shoot someone who doesn't know you. It's *waohola sni,* very ill-bred of you."

"Hee hee hee!" yelped the other in his high laugh. "Ill-bred, eh? Hee hee! That's the spirit, granny. Sure, I will tell you my name. Why not? You're not going to live to repeat it to anyone."

"Oh, excuse me," interrupted the grandmother apologetically. "You misunderstood my meaning. I didn't mean for you to give me *your* name before my grandson hidden behind the window in the log house pulls the trigger of his rifle and shoots you. I hope you will forgive me."

The white man turned the color of a fish that had lain dead too long in the sun of the riverbank. In the stillness that followed, it was Mouse's rifle hammer that made the loud cocking noise. The white man understood that noise. After a long pause, he put his own rifle down on the ground and raised his hands toward the grandmother.

"All right, granny," he said. "You win. My name is Caleb Jabez."

As he spoke, he grinned and sat down on the ground by the fire. It was as though all were friendly now. But the grandmother only nodded watchfully.

"Caleb Jabez," she repeated softly. "Somehow that does not sound just right. Do you have another name, perhaps an Indian name?"

"Of course, I have," said the man, laughing again where there was no reason to laugh. He pointed to the filthy cover of black cloth over his bad eye. "Your people call me from this patch," he explained. "My Indian name is Patch Eye."

At once the old lady brightened. "Ah, yes!" she cried. "Patch Eye Jabez, of course!"

"Aha!" growled the ragged white man. "You've heard *that* name, eh, old hag?"

"No," said the old lady, smiling straight at him. "I never heard it before in my life."

"Granny," said the white man slowly, "are you making a fool of me?"

He was grinning, but his voice was hissing like that of a coiled snake. Watching them from the window, Mouse saw that his left hand was creeping toward his rifle where it lay on the ground beside him. The boy also saw the grandmother did not see the creeping hand. He was about to cry out a desperate warning to her when she suddenly lashed out with her walking cane and brought the knobby stick down upon the white man's outstretched rifle hand. Mouse could hear the knuckle bones crack even from his hiding place. Patch Eye uttered an agonized howl and leaped to his feet, holding and wringing the injured hand, dancing, stomping, and braying aloud like a mule bitten by a rattlesnake on the trail.

As he did so, the old squaw put down her stick and took up once more the small horsehide drum upon which she had been tapping out her prayer-song greeting to the new day. Placing the drum between her knees in the Oglala manner, she began to thump out a perfect accompaniment to the rhythm of the white man's wild jumps and yells, commencing at the same time to chant at the top of her voice the War Dance Song of the Sioux.

Mouse stood up behind the windowsill, his heart swelling with Indian pride. That was *his* grandmother. He touched his fingers to his brow, saluting her.

"*Woyuonihan,* Grandmother!" he shouted. "Your grandson touches his forehead to you!"

Chapter Sixteen

When Patch Eye's hand stopped hurting, he did a strange thing; he laughed and sat down again by the fire.

"All right," he said. "We understand one another. Now to the business. I need a horse. A young one preferably. How much do you want for the colt of many colors there?"

"Heyoka is not for sale," said the old lady. "That's my grandson's pony. He saved the foal's life from Mato."

"I'm sure he's a brave boy, but forget him. I will pay you well for the colt . . . three times his ordinary worth."

"Ah, three times, you say? That's interesting. Mouse!" she called. "Come out here. Our white cousin wishes to buy your little horse. He will pay very high."

Mouse shook his head, not leaving the window. "I heard him, Grandmother. I would not sell Heyoka for forty times his value."

"Oh," grinned the white man, calling to Mouse, "I see you're smart, wise in the head, like your old grandmother. Come out here and let me see you."

"No," said Mouse. "I do not like you."

"Mouse," interrupted the grandmother, "do as Patch Eye says. Otherwise he will think you fear him."

The boy came out of the cabin. He still held the old pony herd rifle, its hammer drawn back to fire. Patch Eye looked him over, then began his whinnying laugh again.

"Hee hee hee!" he chortled. "That is a true grandson of

yours, granny? The runt of the litter, eh? You ought to throw him in on the deal for the bad-colored colt. But I won't be greedy." He turned back to Mouse, his grin fading away. "Well, boy, let us get on with the price. Three times his worth is still what I offer. Thirty iron dollars of the white man. That's a good deal of money for any Indian to have."

The Oglala youth nodded, understanding that this was so. He and the grandmother might live their entire lives on the plains and never see so much money. It was a most difficult thing to decide. The old lady could see that the boy was tempted. She spoke to him quickly, earnestly.

"Mouse, there is something you ought to know before you accept Patch Eye's price. That is why Patch Eye wants the foal."

"Of course," grinned the white man, not hesitating. "It is no secret why I want the colt. I want him to. . . ."

"Wait," commanded the grandmother, holding up her hand. "Go back to the beginning and tell the boy the entire tale. He is a very young boy, not too quick in the head. I myself know very well why you are here and why you want the colt." She paused, dark eyes darting at the white man like swift small birds. "Go on, Patch Eye, tell my grandson why you are here in Big Throat Bridger's place, hunting the great bear."

The white man showed surprise at this shrewd guess. But he quickly narrowed his one eye and accepted the old lady's challenge.

"Well, boy," he shrugged, "I was at Big Throat's fort when Iron Road and some of his people came in to ask Bridger to come up here on Sotoju and kill this black Spirit Bear for them. Bridger told Iron Road he could not leave just then. He was having a fight with the Mormon traders by the Great Salt Lake. He said he was sorry, but that he had no time to go grizzly hunting with Iron Road's Oglalas." Patch Eye paused, smiling at the memory. "Well, your people left the fort and started home very discouraged," he continued. "But they had a better white friend than Big Throat Bridger. It was I, Patch Eye Jabez. So I followed them out on the trail and told them *I* would kill the bear for them, charging them but one half the money they had offered to Big Throat. They agreed soon enough, you may imagine. We shook hands on it and smoked the pipe on it. You know what that means, boy . . . either I kill the bear or those Indians will be looking for my scalp. So now what do you say? Do I get your ribby colt, or don't I? It is for you to decide, but be quick."

He had talked very soberly, seeming in real earnest. Mouse thought he might have misjudged him because he had but one eye and a fierce look, or because he had such a wild coyote's laugh. Perhaps the white man had not actually meant to move his hand toward his rifle on the ground. Also Mouse had his duty to the grandmother. He could not forget her great age. As well, the truth was that Mouse himself was homesick. The summer grew late now. The gray geese were crying high overhead at night, working southward. Soon Wasiya, the Winter Giant, would roar out of the north. The deep snows would come, and Mouse and the grandmother would perish beneath them. Patch Eye seemed to read these hesitations in the young Indian's thoughts.

"Boy," he warned darkly, "unless I kill that bear and free you of his evil spirit, you and granny will not be able to go home to your people this winter. I know the story. Iron Road told it to me. Don't try to lie to me about it."

Mouse turned in desperation to the grandmother. "Help me," he pleaded. "You are old and wise. Tell me what I must do about selling Heyoka, the Clown."

"It is not for me to say," answered the old squaw. "To sell

him or to keep him is your question . . . you must answer it alone."

Now, even more distressed, Mouse turned to Patch Eye. "Perhaps you can help me," he appealed. "If you could tell me what it is you plan to do with my little horse, I might be more content to let you take him. I know it is my duty to sell him for all that money, but my spirit will not agree. It is selfish. It wants me to keep the colt."

Patch Eye Jabez licked his thin lips happily. He fixed his lone eye upon the anxious Oglala youth. "Why, now," he said, lifting his mouth corners into a yellow-toothed smile, "I thought you would have already figured out what I wanted your colt for." He directed the leering grin to the old squaw. "You were right, granny," he said. "Your grandson is not too quick in the head." In an instant the baleful eye was back upon Mouse once more, burning in its red and runny socket like a hot coal. "Think of it in this way, boy," he growled. *"Nothing beats young horseflesh for bear bait."*

Only a white man could have made such a mistake. Mouse felt the anger surge through him. But his words came calmly, as he raised the big pony herd rifle.

"You will leave now," he said, pointing the rifle at Patch Eye's head. "If you have not departed in the time that I count ten, I will pull this trigger."

The boy commenced to count in Sioux. *"Wance, nunpa, yamini* . . . one, two, three. . . ."

Patch Eye frowned uncertainly and looked at the grandmother. Beneath its grime of camp dirt and black stubble, his face grew pale. "Granny," he asked, "would the boy really do it?"

"I don't know," shrugged the old squaw. "However, you might remember that he is an Oglala. You yourself said that tribe was not too loving toward the white man."

Patch Eye cursed loudly in his own language, then became quiet, watching Mouse. Mouse was continuing to count out loud in the Oglala tongue.

"Zeptan, sakape, sakowin," said the boy. "Five, six, seven. . . ."

At "seven" the white man spat into the fire and cursed again, glaring at Mouse. "Go ahead, runt," he sneered. "Keep counting. You haven't the nerve to shoot anybody."

The boy nodded. *"Sakalohan, napiciyunka,"* he said. "Eight, nine. . . ."

Patch Eye threw up his hands hurriedly. "Wait!" he cried. "That's far enough. You needn't say ten. I am leaving as you said."

He gave the Indian boy a last look. It was the look in the eyes of a dog sick with the foaming-mouth disease. In it was the shadow of death, and with it the white man returned his words to the grandmother.

"Old woman," he growled, "I go in peace, but I must request one favor. No man can stay alive in this country without his rifle. May I pick up the Kentucky rifle?"

For answer, the grandmother left the fire and picked up the long rifle herself. Limping over to Patch Eye's waiting horse, she put the weapon into its saddle scabbard upside down, the muzzle pointing to the sky. Going back to the fireside, she got the coffee pot and poured its steaming contents down the barrel of the Kentucky rifle.

"There." She smiled, giving the rifle a pat. "Now let us see how well you can spit out a bullet with that nice wet gunpowder in your gullet."

She hobbled over to Patch Eye, speaking quietly to him.

"You must think that we are great fools, the grandson and I, but we are not. *Now* you can go in peace. Get out."

Patch Eye got on his horse, saying nothing. He sat a moment in the saddle, looking down at the two small Indians who had bested him. Mouse was certain he was going to snarl some vicious threat against their lives, but he did not do so. Instead he laughed.

"Well, good hunting, cousins," he said, turning his horse away with a friendly wave. *"I will be back."*

Mouse watched him ride off across the meadow and out of sight down the waterfall trail to the outer valley. The white man did not once glance back. Mouse felt very uneasy.

"Do you think he *will* come back, Grandmother?" he asked.

"Of course," answered the old lady. "He will come back because he wants your young horse to bait the bear with. If he must do so in order to steal Heyoka, he will also cut our throats in our sleep, or send a bullet through us from ambush. That is the reputation he has. Why that old fool Iron Road ever did business with him, the gods alone know."

Mouse looked at her for a long moment. She looked back at him for another long moment.

"Grandmother," murmured the boy, crouching to the fire, "I am much afraid."

"Boy," sighed the wrinkled squaw, sinking down beside him, "let me tell you something . . . so is your old grandmother!"

Chapter Seventeen

Days passed swiftly. A particular night came in which there was a great stillness, and the moon shone with unusual brightness. It was in the middle of this night that Sunsunla, grazing on the old cabin's sod roof, suddenly uttered his raucous warning bray. It was a sound rude enough to awaken the spirits of the departed. The grandmother leaped from her bed, ran to the open window.

"Mouse," she whispered, "come quickly. Bring the rifle. Someone is out there among our ponies."

They had built a pen for the animals since Patch Eye's threat to return. Each night they drove the ponies, including Heyoka, into this pen, which could easily be seen from the window of the house. This was so that Mouse might aim Old Caniyassa out of the window and fire it at anyone bothering their animals. Now the boy scrambled from his sleeping robe to join the grandmother.

When he peered out into the moonlight, however, he could see nothing amiss at the pen. Their old ponies were standing in it as quietly as usual. But wait, there was something wrong.

"Grandmother," said Mouse fearfully, "I don't see Heyoka out there."

"Well, don't be alarmed," cautioned the old lady, peering harder. "He is probably standing behind one of the mares. Come on, we'll go out there and make sure. You will see that I am right."

Mouse went with her, but his heart was already weeping. Some instinct told him that Heyoka was gone. And he was. In the brilliant light of the moon they could see the foal's trim hoof prints leading away from the pen. Moreover, with the tracks of the orphan wild foal were those of another horse, one which both boy and grandmother knew well.

"I was wrong," said the old lady in a low voice. "Those are the hoof marks of Patch Eye's pony. I am sorry, Mouse. Your little colt is gone."

At first the youth wept, then in anger turned on Sunsunla, the mule. "It is your fault!" he raged, shaking his fist up at the ancient beast. "Why didn't you bray sooner? Wait until I get my driving stick, you miserable Donkey!"

"Wait, wait," advised the grandmother, taking him by the arm. "The mule did his best. If he had not warned us, Patch Eye might have slit our throats as well as stolen your colt."

That was a possibility the boy had forgotten. Thinking of it he lost his anger. "I am sorry, mule," he apologized. "Come on down from the roof. I won't hit you with the stick."

Sunsunla scrambled down and came over to the boy. He placed his great homely muzzle against his shoulder and made a soft noise in his throat. From the beginning the old mule and the foundling wild colt had been comrades. It was the bony white mare that, having lost her own foal, had suckled Heyoka to his weaning age. But it had been the ragged mule, Sunsunla, that the spraddle-legged foal had adored. Now Mouse understood that the mule was sharing his grief for the loss of a common loved one. The boy began to weep again.

But the old grandmother had a disposition with more salt in it. She pushed Sunsunla aside, patted Mouse on the back. "Now, now, boy," she said. "No more of that. Dry your eyes. Let this be a lesson to both of us. We ought to have taken

Patch Eye's money. We were fools. Thirty iron dollars! Think of it."

She had never felt about Heyoka as had her grandson. To her the foal had been only another mouth to feed where she and Mouse were poor as field mice already, and had to worry each day about filling their own bellies. But to the boy the foal had been everything. He had meant more to Mouse than had Fox or Turtle or Bald Head, or even Mato Sapa. Only the grandmother herself had stood as high in the boy's heart as the orphan foal, Heyoka. Now the little horse was gone, lost to a terrible fate. It was more than his master could abide.

"Grandmother," he said tremblingly, "I cannot let Clown go to be used as bear bait, yet I do not have the courage to go after him. What must I do?"

"Courage, you say?" snorted the old lady. "Do you mean that because a little boy of thirteen summers is afraid to go after a white man and an Indian-hater with a bad reputation that this makes the boy a coward? Nonsense. You would be a fool, and a dead fool, to try to follow Patch Eye."

"Yes, but what must I do, Grandmother?"

"You will have to let the colt go, Mouse. We must think first of ourselves. If we permit Patch Eye to keep the colt, then perhaps he will leave us alone. Perhaps he will also have good hunting luck and succeed in luring Mato into the bait and killing him. Then you and I would be free to go home down the mountain before the big snows come."

"That may be, Grandmother, but Heyoka will be dead."

"Boy," admonished the old lady, "we cannot fight the white man. Not this white man or any white man. The white man takes what he cannot pay for, and he will not pay for what he can take. He has treated the Indian in this manner since I have known him, and this is a long time, thirty-five and more winters. Nothing changes. We are Indians. Patch

Eye is a white man. Even if you followed him and by some good fortune shot him with your pony herd rifle, the other white men would come and take you and put a long rope about your neck and pull you up into a tree and dangle you there until all the breath was gone from your body. *Ai-eee!*"

She made Mouse angry with her talk at the same time that she made him sad for her. She was of the old ways. She hated the white man and did not try to understand him. But Mouse did not hate the white man, even though he held such great fear of Patch Eye Jabez. So he calmed himself and patted the old lady's hand.

"All right, Grandmother," he said. "It will be as you say. We will forget the colt. We will let him go."

"*Waste*, good," said the old squaw, shivering. "Come on, boy, it's cold out here in this night air. Let us return to our warm beds."

They went into the log house and sought their sleeping places. Waiting until the grandmother's snores were rising steadily, Mouse climbed out of his tattered buffalo robe. Quickly he made his preparations, doing what his courage told him must be done. When all was ready, he stole over and kissed the grandmother on her withered cheek.

"Good bye, old lady," he whispered. "Pray for your grandson when you wake up and find him gone."

Chapter Eighteen

Mouse and Sunsunla went through the darkness toward the lower waterfall. It was that part of the dawn when the deer had quit feeding, the coyote given his last yip, when the moon had set but the stars still shone overhead. It was so quiet that the hoofs of Sunsunla, pushing through the dewy meadow grasses, made a sound as though wading in shallow water.

The boy had chosen the old mule to be his mount because he was wiser than any horse. Also he was stronger, could go farther on less to eat, and would faithfully follow the track line of his friend, Heyoka. A mule was much like a dog; he would remember his friends. Horses forgot each other in little time. Mouse had as well for equipment on the trail his ragged blanket, axe, knife, small hunting bow, and, of course, Old Caniyassa, the pony herd rifle with its single load of scrap iron and lead.

At the place below the falls where Mouse and the grandmother had made the noon halting on the day of discovering the log house, the boy spoke to the mule.

"We will wait here for the full daylight," he said. "On such rocky ground we might miss Heyoka's tracks in this poor light."

Sunsunla began to graze along the creekbank, leaving his master to huddle in the dark listening to the cold rush of the stream. It seemed to the boy as if daylight would never come.

His courage commenced to shrink. Other things marched through his mind.

He had left the grandmother asleep. She would miss the mule and the rifle and would know Mouse had gone after Heyoka. But would she understand? Would she bless her grandson? Had Mouse done right to desert an old woman high in the mountains with winter coming? Where did his real duty lie? With the old grandmother or the young horse? Both were his family. Both loved him and he them.

Then there was Mato. How did Mouse feel about him? Did he really want to see that Lord of the Mountain parted from his brave spirit? Would he pay that price just to have his and the grandmother's bodies freed of Mato's spirit so they might go home to their people? Mouse did not know. It was true that he was homesick. He longed for his friends. He was lonesome for his work of guarding the pony herd. From this view he should pray for Patch Eye to kill the bear, yet he was not certain. One thing of which he was sure, however, was that winter was coming very swiftly. If the snows caught the old lady and him, *ai-eee!* that would be the end of it all.

At last the daylight grew strong enough to depart. Mouse clambered up on Sunsunla. The mule lumbered off in his awkward, stiff trot. They followed the track lines of Heyoka and Patch Eye's horse. Mouse only sat on Sunsunla's back, saying nothing; the old mule knew where he was going.

From time to time the boy would stop and climb a tall tree to study the land ahead, lest Patch Eye be hiding to ambush them. But the white man did not even stop to look back. At noon, he halted to make coffee and that was all. By nightfall he had ridden entirely around the lower end of the valley and come back to a place directly across the central meadow from the little house of logs. With the last of the sunlight, Mouse had looked for the grandmother over there but had not seen her. The small cabin seemed deserted.

As for Patch Eye's campsite, he chose it carelessly. After all, he had no fear of being followed. Not by an undersized boy and a crippled old woman. Especially when both were Indians and far, far from their people.

Mouse, meanwhile, had other convictions. When it was fully dark, he tied Sunsunla in a patch of alder brush where he could not be seen. Leaving the mule, he crept along the mountainside until he lay immediately above the campfire of Patch Eye. He was so close to it that he could plainly smell the delicious odor of the young rabbit that the white man was broiling for his supper. The very nearness made the Oglala youth shake with nerves. He had to clench his teeth and lecture himself: *Now, Mouse, you must be brave or Heyoka will never come away with his life. Breathe lightly and do not move one muscle. Have the courage of the grandmother. An idea will then come to you by which you can defeat Patch Eye and set Heyoka free.*

This good advice was interrupted by Patch Eye's voice. Like Mouse the white man was talking to himself. Yet unlike the Oglala boy, he was talking out loud. People did this when in lonely country, Mouse knew, the Indian as much as the white man. But people still did not like to admit that they did talk to themselves. That was what crazy people did. So the other people would make believe they were talking to their horse, or to a friendly chipmunk on a nearby rock, or to a noisy blue jay begging for a scrap of food. This was what Patch Eye Jabez was doing now.

"Well, here we are," the black-bearded hunter began. He spat out the last rabbit bone and took up his coffee cup. "Tomorrow we will find our baiting tree and get started. I can smell snow in the air, and we are going to have to get this bear

in a hurry. You there!" he called to Heyoka. "Do you understand me, you Oglala scrub?"

The colt whickered and pricked his ears.

"Oh, you do, eh?" Patch Eye leered. "Let me tell you a bit
more, then. Perhaps it will make you not so happy."

He went on to describe in detail why Mato would be so
pleased to find Heyoka tied under the baiting tree. The
summer had been exceedingly dry, he said. The driest in
many moons. No good berries had grown on the *wica kanaska*
bushes. The earth had been too hard for digging the edible
roots of the *tinpsila* and the *siptola*. Even the seeds of the
pangi, the sunflower, were scarce. The fat ground squirrels
and field mice had migrated to lower meadows and fresher
forage. After them had gone most of the great bears in the
valley, leaving Mato alone. The great bear had stayed because his hatred of the Indians was greater than the hunger of
his belly and because this high valley was *his* valley, and he
would not be driven from it. But now at last the Lord Grizzly
was to have a fitting meal.

"Hee hee hee!" concluded the hunter, "you will see tomorrow, homely colt. All that the Oglala boy will ever find of
you will be a pile of clean bones and four hoofs. If the bear is
hungry enough, he may even eat the four hoofs, also. How
does that sound to you, young horse?" He paused to laugh
again. "You think you will whicker in your friendly way when
the black one comes sniffing toward you where you are tied
on the tether rope? Can't you just see him now, with his huge
nose in the air, swinging back and forth to follow your sweet
scent? Ah, but don't worry. You will have company up there
in the Land of the Shadows before long. Those Oglalas are
not going to make a fool of Caleb Jabez. The old woman and
her skinny grandson will see me again. And when they do,
then is when you will be getting that company up there in

Wanagi Yata. They'll meet you up there, never fear . . . hee hee hee hee!"

It was then that Mouse understood that Patch Eye Jabez was crazy. The *real* crazy, not the rambling happy kind of crazy such as the old grandmother. It was then, too, that the Sioux youth understood what he must do there from his rocky hiding place upon the mountainside. There was no choice remaining to him, and no other chance. *He must kill Patch Eye Jabez.*

Chapter Nineteen

Noiselessly Mouse raised Old Caniyassa to his shoulder. Slowly he drew the stock of the pony herd rifle tightly to his cheek. His sighting eye narrowed along the dull brown barrel of the ancient musket. His aim came to bear upon the breast of Patch Eye. His finger tensed on the trigger. To himself the boy prayed: *May Wakan Tanka guide this messenger, forgiving he who sends it forth by need alone*. Yet the messenger was never sent.

Mouse's finger would not make the final pressure upon the rifle's trigger. Gradually he lowered Old Caniyassa; in the final instant of truth he could not shoot anyone from hiding, could not send that terrible loading of jagged iron scraps into even Patch Eye Jabez.

Still the boy knew that, if he could *not* kill the white man in cold blood, he yet must save his colt, Heyoka, from him. There was but one other way to do it. He must steal the colt, and he must do it that very night, from those very rocks among which he crouched.

In this regard he had some luck. Patch Eye was full of broiled rabbit and very drowsy. He fell asleep in a brief time. His bony saddle horse also dropped its head and went to whatever dreamland old ponies prefer. Even Heyoka dozed off quickly. The fire died away to a glow of red coals. The night drew in all about the silent campsite.

Mouse slid out the knife with which he would cut the

tether rope of Heyoka. He put the blade between his teeth, leaving his hands free for crawling. Old Caniyassa he left among the rocks. Wriggling on his stomach he started down the mountainside. Past the fire he went, past Patch Eye Jabez who snored beside it. Nearing the place where the colt was tied, the boy held his breath and froze stiff as a hiding fawn. A wandering breeze had stirred the ashes of the fire, swirled on along the ground over Mouse and toward the sleeping Heyoka. Immediately the colt aroused, the familiar scent of his master in his nostrils. Eagerly he shot his ears forward seeking the whereabouts of his friend, Tonkalla. Mouse prayed, but it did no good. Heyoka saw him there on the ground. The colt's whinny of welcome would have awakened a hibernating bear; its piercing high sound struck Patch Eye with the force of a fired arrow.

The white man rolled sideways toward his Kentucky rifle. Seizing the weapon, he aimed it across the embers at Mouse and fired it in a fragment of time smaller than the Oglala boy required even to think about jumping up and running for his life.

The very nearness and quickness of the shot provided a second chance to the Indian youth, however. Mouse felt the blast of the powder flame scorch his face. It was so close that he could smell the burned hair of his eyebrows. Yet by some miracle the bullet itself missed him, only grazing one of his ears. Leaping to his feet, Mouse bounded away toward the rocks above.

Diving into the rocks, Mouse scooped up Old Caniyassa and ran on. The foul oaths of Patch Eye lent speed to the lad's feet and for a time he believed that he would out-distance the white man, even carrying the heavy old pony herd rifle. But Patch Eye's skill to run a trail through the night by the sounds of his fleeing quarry was as that of a hunting wolf. As Mouse neared the alder clump in which he had left Sunsunla, the bearded bear trapper was only a stride or two behind him. He was so close, indeed, that Mouse knew nothing else to do except to try diving in under the dozing mule. In this way he thought to gain a moment in which to shoulder and aim Old Caniyassa at his pursuer, but the desperate idea provided an even greater reward.

As the boy slid in under Sunsunla, Patch Eye made a wild lunge to seize the youth, not seeing the old mule at all! The white man's head slammed into Sunsunla's ribs, driving a grunt of rude surprise from the ancient beast. With an indignant bray, Sunsunla gathered up his heels and let them fly into the middle of Patch Eye's body. A yell of great pain rent the night. Propelled by the mule's tremendous kick, Patch Eye's ragged form landed with a belly-flat splash in the scum water and mud of a nearby beaver pond.

Mouse listened fearfully, but heard no sound except the lapping of the disturbed waters. Soon even that died away. Re-gathering his courage, the Oglala boy made preparation to depart before Patch Eye might recover.

Untying Sunsunla, he placed Old Caniyassa in its leather cover and fastened the weapon to the mule's girth strap so that it would not be lost along the trail should a gallop be required in their escape. The boy's mind was already reaching ahead to the rescue, also, of little Heyoka. With Patch Eye floating, unconscious in the beaver pond—or, perhaps, even worse off than that—Mouse knew that he and the old mule could reach the deserted campfire of the white man and free their friend the Clown with no great difficulty. They might have time to take along Patch Eye's pony as well, leaving the white man on foot and helpless to catch them.

"Come on," the lad whispered to Sunsunla, "let us get far away from here, old mule. *Hookahey!*"

He seized the faithful animal's halter with one hand, reached with the other hand for his bristly mane to swing himself up on the mule's back. It was in that moment that Patch Eye's voice spoke out of the darkness.

"Sioux boy," the injured white man said, each word revealing the pain of his bruised bones, "that was a pretty trick, leading me into the mule's heels. Yet I have a prettier trick to pay you back for it. *Watch out for it, boy.*"

That was all, just those few words in Sioux, hissed in withering anger out of the darkness. But Mouse could not control his terror at hearing them; the Oglala boy had no more courage remaining.

He dropped the halter of Sunsunla and fled into the night on foot, abandoning the old mule in his blind fright. He ran like a crazed animal. Trees became ghosts reaching out to snare him. Rocks turned into crouching beasts waiting to spring for his throat. He did not even realize in which direction he fled. But Patch Eye could hear him, and the white man was waiting for him when the Indian boy blundered out of the alder bush onto the open mountainside. Mouse ran straight into his great hairy arms.

The fright of the capture was too great. The small form collapsed and fell unconscious.

Chapter Twenty

When Mouse regained consciousness, he was again in the camp of Patch Eye. He was tightly bound by rope, and, since it had rained during his "sleep," the boy was shivering with cold. Over eastward, where the grandmother would yet be slumbering in their log house, the sky was turning gray. Soon it would be morning. By the fire Patch Eye sat frying some fat salt pork in an iron pan. The coffee pot hung on its spit, steaming. Mouse, who had not eaten the entire day, felt his mouth water to the fragrant aromas. Yet he remained very quiet, not wishing Patch Eye to know he was awake once more.

The white man was in a strange mood—happy. He whistled a foolish small tune of his people as he sniffed the pork sizzling in its delicious greases. But suddenly his single eye rolled in the direction of his captive. The whistle stopped abruptly.

"*Hohahe,* welcome to my teepee." He grinned at the Sioux youth. He spread his hands to indicate the campsite. "The roof leaks when it rains, but otherwise everything is *owanyeke waste,* eh?"

Mouse shivered again and blew a raindrop from the tip of his nose. "Patch Eye," he said, "what are you going to do with me? And with my colt, Heyoka?"

Patch Eye grinned, bit into a piece of juicy hot pork. "Well, now, Oglala boy, those are good questions. What do you think their answers will be?"

"Will you kill both of us?" asked the youth.

Patch Eye spat out a shred of pork gristle and reached to fill his coffee cup. "Not me," he answered.

Somehow the way in which he uttered the denial did not relieve Mouse's anxiety. "I think that my grandmother would take the thirty iron dollars at this time," he offered hopefully. "That is, if you still wish to buy the little horse. Do you want me to go across the valley and ask her?"

"Hee hee hee!" laughed the white man. "You are a very funny Indian."

Mouse had not intended to be humorous. Now, however, seeing the foolishness of his proposal, he withdrew it. "Very well"—he nodded, blowing away another raindrop—"but please spare the colt. I will do anything you say to save his life. I will even take his place beneath the bear-bait tree, if only you will set Heyoka free."

Patch Eye Jabez stopped eating and stared at him. His ferocious grin began to uncover his teeth. He laughed wildly, and as quickly ceased. The wolfish grin faded. "You've made a deal, boy," he said. "I *will* use you for bait under that bear tree."

Mouse's heart failed at the cold words. It was difficult to appear brave about being a bear bait, but, after all, it would save Heyoka and that was what he had set out to do. "Thank you," he said. "I am happy for my little horse."

Patch Eye continued eating. He made no move to free Heyoka. Mouse felt a chill grow inside his stomach. "White man," he said determinedly, "a bargain is a bargain. Please to set my colt free so that he may return to the grandmother. He's a smart colt. He will find his way home safely. Or do you mean to go back on your word?"

Patch Eye's thick lips once more lifted in a snarling twist of a grin. His lone eye rolled in its socket. "Caleb Jabez go back on his word, boy? Never!" he said. "What I promise to do, I do. And what I promised you was a better trick than your mule kicking in my ribs. So here is the trick."

He poured himself another cup of coffee, leaned forward with a leer. Mouse's stomach grew colder still.

"Now this black grizzly I am after." Patch Eye grinned. "He's a savage one and very clever. I can settle his stew with my Kentucky rifle, but first I have to beat him with my own cunning. I have to get him to come in to the bait where I can hit him with the rifle.

"Even after stealing your colt for bait, I have worried that this bear was too smart. He knows I came into this valley with one horse, the old one. He probably knows that this young horse is yours and the old lady's. He's easily that cagey, don't think he isn't. He has no doubt looked over your log cabin and all your livestock long ago.

"So I figured I was going to have trouble until you came up with that bright idea a moment ago. You know, the old bear would not like the looks of your colt without *you* to go along with him. Now everything will look natural to him, eh, boy? You *and* your colt under the tree together! Hee hee!"

Mouse could not answer, and the white man laughed again.

"Aha!" he said, winking his watery eye. "You begin to see the bargain now, eh? How do you like it? You think it's as good a trick as leading me into that mule's heels?"

The Indian youth sat, silent in his bonds, the cold rain dripping from him. What a cruel thing for Wakan Tanka to permit to fall upon his red child, Tonkalla, and the faithful colt, Heyoka. It was more than a boy of thirteen summers could endure. When Mouse lowered his head in despair, it was not only rain that ran down his cheeks. Still he did his best to hide the weakness from Patch Eye. Even when he knew he would be tied beside his own pony as grizzly bear bait, an Oglala did not care to have a white man see him weep.

Chapter Twenty-One

Patch Eye tied the boy on his own bony horse. He tied Heyoka on a rope behind the bony horse. They set out up the valley, Patch Eye leading the way on foot.

It was still early, a few stars yet showing faintly. The rain fell now and again. Low clouds scudded over the valley ahead of a cold wind. Mouse looked to the east. He could see the coming daylight touching the underbellies of the dark clouds. Lightning flashed in that direction. Becoming nervous, Heyoka whinnied and trotted up to rub his head against the old bony horse and whicker at Mouse in low mustang noises that the boy understood.

"Be calm, little horse," he said. "Don't be afraid. Remember we are both Oglalas, you and I."

Patch Eye Jabez glanced back at them. "I heard that," he growled. "Let's wait and see how brave you Oglalas are when you are both tied under the bait tree and old Mato comes sniffing down the wind following your scent. Hee hee hee! Too bad I won't be there."

"You won't be there?" echoed Mouse, surprised. "Have you decided not to shoot over the bait? You have a better plan to get the bear?"

"Much better," answered Patch Eye.

They had come to a place where the trail dropped down a steep granite ledge into a small meadow completely surrounded by tall dark pines.

"You see that meadow?" the white man continued. "That is where you and your paint-pot-colored colt are going to sleep your last sleep. But not just yet. We must be careful with this bear. I don't want him to see us too soon."

"What do you mean, Patch Eye?"

"It's too soon to go down to the meadow. We will hide up here in the rocks until the right time."

He led the old horse and Heyoka into the cover of some huge boulders back from the ledge. There he spread his greasy blankets, one beneath him, one over him to shed the rain. The Oglala boy he left tied on the horse, not covering him in any way. All the long day they waited in the rocks. There was no eating, no smoking, no talking. Just the sitting and the waiting. Finally sundown neared.

Patch Eye stood up and rolled his blankets. "The light is about right down there now," he said to the boy. "Just time enough before the sun goes down for me to make you and your colt comfortable for the night, eh?"

Mouse was so stiff and weary from his bonds that he could scarcely reply. But the white man had the wild look in his face again, and the boy believed it best not to cross him.

"If you say so," he answered.

They went down into the meadow then, moving quickly, yet with caution. Patch Eye searched the edges of the open grass looking for just the right place. Finally he seemed to have found it.

"Here," he said, "this will do, just under these tall pines here where the trail comes down from the higher country."

He cut the ropes from Mouse's feet, lifted the boy down from the horse. Mouse's legs crumpled beneath him. He could not stand up from being bound so many hours. Patch Eye made no effort to help him up again. Instead, he took from the pack behind the old horse's saddle a long object rolled in antelope skin.

"Do you recognize this?" he said to the helpless youth. "Your people gave it to me."

Mouse indicated that he did not know what the object might be. Patch Eye nodded and unrolled the antelope skin. Inside it was a short Sioux buffalo lance, painted ghostly white with the Katela symbol—the death sign—painted three times in black upon the haft. Mouse's eyes widened.

"It's the sacred lance, the spirit killer," he breathed in wonderment.

"It is," said Patch Eye Jabez. "Now you know why your people gave it to me, eh?"

"Yes. You must drive it through Mato's heart so that his evil spirit will die with him and not escape to roam again in some other bear. But you must do it while he yet lives, not after he dies by your bullets. It will not work if he is already dead."

"Aye, that's it. Your cursed people! They would not permit me simply to shoot the bear and collect my money. They won't trust my word on it, either. Old Iron Road will likely send a party of braves up here to check on the kill when I have made it. If they find their bear full of bullet holes, they would want their money back. They might even want to charge me a little something extra, eh, Oglala boy? Let us say like my long black scalp lock whacked off with a buffalo skinning knife. *Ai-eee!* Hee hee hee hee!"

Mouse shook his head frowningly. "But how will you kill mighty Mato with that tiny stick?" he asked, pointing at the sacred lance with a nod of his head. "You would not even be able to draw near him with such a weapon. You intend to cheat my people in some way?"

"Never!" The white man laughed. "When I draw near the bear, I will have him safely in a *wikmunke,* just as I have you and your precious colt!"

"A trap?" said Mouse. "You mean to catch that great bear in a simple trap?"

"Well, you surely don't expect me to catch him in a rainbow, do you?"

Wikmunke was, of course, the Sioux word for either a trap or a rainbow, but Mouse did not appreciate Patch Eye's small joke just then.

"What kind of a trap?" he asked, praying the sun would set the slowest it ever had, lingering long enough for Mato to see them in the meadow and go away. "A special trap?"

For answer, the white man went again to the pack behind the saddle. He removed from it a heavy bundle in a burlap sack, which Mouse had thought to be the food sack. But it held no food. In it was a giant of all bear traps. The teeth of the jaws surrounding the bait pan were so ragged and deeply cut they would hold any bear. The chain was as thick as a man's forearms. Black Mato was in grave danger, and Mouse suddenly felt a great pity for the bear.

"Patch Eye," he said, "you are the one with the evil spirit in you, not Mato."

"That's right, boy," said the white man. "And the evil mind to go with it, too. You'll see."

Swiftly he went to work. He tied Heyoka on a grazing rope exactly as a Sioux boy would tie his pony in such a camping place. Mouse, he bound to four stakes driven into the ground nearby, a gag in his mouth so that he would not cry out to warn the bear, or try to frighten him with the sound of human words. After that, he covered the Indian boy with his small ragged blanket, making it appear as if the youth slept while his pony fed in the meadow grass beside him. It was all very cleverly done, but Patch Eye had only commenced to show his evil cunning.

There was a natural path, or trail way, leading down into

the meadow from the great mountain above. Mouse had studied this track already, having recognized it for a game path of some variety. Now the white man grinned as he pointed up along the worn thoroughfare and spoke to the Oglala boy.

"Mato's road," he told him. "There is where it ends high up there on Sotoju. The split cliff trail which enters the valley is not the road's true ending. Where we are looking up the mountain is Mato's true home. You see the bare rocks far beyond the dark pine trees? You mark that great cañon wall which ends among the topmost snows of Sotoju? Up there where the white winds blow forever? Well, your great bear lives up there. He is up there this moment. I know he is. I have watched him for many days. He has gone up there to his high place to wait until I have left the valley. Only when he sees me go, will he come down."

Mouse said nothing. But a slender hope was growing in his imagination. Patch Eye pounced on it like a panther.

"Hee hee!" he cried. "You are thinking that, if this is the case and since I am still here, he will not come down, eh? Hah, I am not that simple, Indian boy. I will make the bear come. I will leave the valley. I will go now as soon as I have set the trap. He will see me go, for he is watching me this moment from up there. Hee hee hee!"

Patch Eye got his battered short shovel from his pack.

"When the bear sees me set out straight across the valley toward the trail through the cliff, he will come down to smell around where I have been and make sure that I am gone. When he does that, the first thing which will sting his hungry nose will be the hot sweet smell of your young colt! *Ih,* do you agree?"

Mouse rolled his eyes, unable to reply because of the gag in his mouth.

"Well, never mind, it will come to you!" Patch Eye grinned and set to work.

He dug a hole in Mato's road precisely where the bear would come along it down the mountain into the meadow. He put into this hole the gigantic trap, covering it skillfully with pine needles. He then drove an iron stake into a huge dead log and fastened the trap chain to the stake.

"There," announced the ragged hunter, "by the time old Mato has dragged that log up the mountain a mile or so, he will be so weak a child could put the holy lance into him."

Again Mouse rolled his eyes, the silent fear mounting within him. Tonkalla was doomed. Heyoka was doomed. Mato was doomed. It was a time for praying.

Patch Eye mounted his old horse, whistling and singing very loudly. He seemed to be making a very great deal of noise of a sudden, and belatedly Mouse realized why. The hunter wanted Mato to know that he was leaving the meadow. He wanted to be certain the bear was watching and listening when he rode off toward the distant exit of the cliff trail.

"Well, good luck, boy!" Patch Eye waved pleasantly. He scratched his tangled beard, spat tobacco juice into the grass. "Give my best to Mato when he comes down to see you this evening. You'll have somewhat of a wait, I believe, but he will be here, never fear. Look for him about firefly time. Early twilight. First dusk. That's when grizzlies come a-calling. Don't worry meanwhile. If I see old granny along the trail, I'll tell her what a brave Oglala you were. You and your paint-pot colt. *Wagh!*"

Wagh was the Indian word for the sound the great grizzly bears made when they were angry or deeply wounded. The Sioux employed it as a courage word. Their warriors shouted it in battle to give to one another the strength and power of the king of bears. It was especially used when the battle went badly, when victory seemed impossible, when only some miracle could save the fight.

Mouse knew how Patch Eye had meant it: that nothing could save Heyoka and him. The boy could still hear the crazed white man laughing his wild laugh long after he had disappeared into the dark pines and Heyoka and he were left alone in the silent meadow to wait for twilight and the great black bear that would come, with the night, down off the mountain.

Chapter Twenty-Two

A hundred despairs darkened Mouse's imagination. The sunset had long faded. An hour had fled since Patch Eye's departure. The evening hush was deeply fallen upon the mountainside. Twilight closed in swiftly.

The boy suffered beneath the sodden blanket. His ankles and wrists were worn raw where he had struggled against the stake ropes. His back ached as though with many small knife wounds. Hunger and thirst assailed him, especially thirst, for he had drunk nothing save the rainwater that had fallen upon his face. Yet, finally, it was his heart that hurt him most sorely. Each time that he looked at Heyoka, grazing contentedly at his tether's end, the Indian boy knew real pain. When the many-colored colt would raise his head and whicker in his trusting way—letting his young master know that all was well with the world—then the hurting in Mouse's breast became as an arrow wound.

With the sun gone at last and the mountain air grown cold with the sharpness of the September Moon, the boy tried once more to think of some way in which he might win freedom for the colt and himself. His thoughts turned naturally to the old grandmother. Perhaps the old lady, missing her grandson for so long a time, had started out to find him. Ah, but then of what use could that be now? The rain of the day had washed out all trail signs from Patch Eye's camp to the meadow. Even should the ancient squaw have come as far as the camp, before the rain, where could she turn past that place? The answer was no place at all.

All right, Sunsunla, the mule, then. Was it possible the faithful brute might have escaped the alder clump after Mouse let go of his halter to flee into the arms of Patch Eye? The white man had refused to answer this question for the boy. When Mouse had asked him what happened to the old mule, he had only laughed and told the boy not to worry about mules, that bears were what he ought to be thinking about! Mouse feared that Patch Eye had trailed and shot the mule out of anger for Sunsunla's kicking him. He could have done this while the boy lay unconscious, for Mouse in truth had no least idea how long he had "slept" following his fainting from fright in Patch Eye's hairy grasp. Also the old mule might be free this moment. Free and sneaking around out in the pine trees looking for Mouse and Heyoka in the dark. But then the boy knew this was a foolish hope. What might a mule do to unfasten stake ropes? Or to fight off grizzly bears? No, forget Sunsunla. Pray he might yet be alive somewhere, but expect no more help from him than from the grandmother.

That left only Patch Eye Jabez himself. Well, what about the black-bearded hunter? Was he as cruel as he seemed? Or was he merely trying to earn Iron Road's money, trying to help the Oglala people by killing the bear they feared so greatly? Was he really only using Mouse to make Heyoka seem a natural bait, a pony grazing beside his sleeping master, and not tied to lure the bear within shooting range of the Kentucky rifle? Did he believe the boy would be safe, even if the bear took the colt? Yes, surely, that *could* be it. Mouse knew that bears would not touch human flesh where any other was available. Did Patch Eye think to depend upon this fact in his plan to bring the great bear into the buried trap in

Mato's road? Yes, yes, thought the desperate youth. That must be it! Patch Eye would return when Mato was in the trap and free both Heyoka and Mouse unharmed, letting all end well.

Except for one thing. Or two things. What if Mato did *not* get caught in the trap? What if he came around the trap and killed Heyoka and dragged the colt away for his supper, as he had done with old Rainbow, the colt's mother? What then?

Patch Eye could not stay on any longer to hunt the great bear. The big snows were coming more surely than ever now. Mouse had smelled them all day in the rainy wind. No, the hunter might never return. If the trap missed seizing Mato with its ragged teeth, the white man would surely go on out of the valley and down the mountain. Faithful to Mouse, the poor grandmother would not leave the valley, however, until she had found the boy. Not finding him, she would freeze in the little house of logs, or starve for lack of food. Mouse himself would linger in the ropes that bound him to the stakes. Heyoka would furnish the last feast for Mato Sapa before that great king of all the grizzly bears retired into his granite cave to sleep the winter through. Not even Mato would come back to see Mouse.

As for Sunsunla, the ragged-eared rascal was easily smart enough to find his way out of the valley through the dark cliff trail. He, no more than Mato, would return to bid farewell to Mouse. Only the wind and the snow and the cold stars of September would say good bye to him. And in the springtime, when the sunflowers came again, the skies of summer following would look down upon three piles of lonely Oglala bones. They would be Heyoka's and the grandmother's and his own.

It was as the dismal prospect arose in his mind that the boy heard the colt's sharply warning snort. Mouse, squinting through the night, saw the young horse prick his ears and flare his nostrils. His eyes were showing the white rim of fear all around. He was staring off as though he had scented a ghost through the purple dusk.

Mouse forced his own eyes to travel past the nervous colt and to move along the shadowed trail of Mato's road beyond the place where Patch Eye had buried the trap. The boy knew sheer terror then. Mato had come down to the bait. He was standing up there in the dark watching Mouse.

Mouse could just make him out, a gigantic black shadow against the twilight gloom of the mountain behind him. His head swung to and fro, searching the evening breeze. The boy heard him grunt softly, and knew he had scented the colt. Turning his gaze from him a moment to see how Heyoka was reacting, he looked back to find the trail empty. Mato had disappeared.

Mouse blinked hard. Could it have been his imagination playing tricks upon him? But no, shadows did not grunt and blow out softly through their nostrils. The boy shook with fear. Rolling his head as far as his bonds would permit, he scanned the edges of the meadow. Nothing there. Wait. What was that? Over there beyond Heyoka. In the blackness of the pines. Just where the trail came down from the mountain. It was Mato.

Now the colt saw him. His ears shot forward; his nostrils flared. He bunched his hindquarters, squatting like a frightened rabbit. Then he was bawling with fear. He made a mustang noise that whistled wildly. He reared and lashed the air with his hoofs. He lunged to the end of the tether rope, neighing frantically. But the rope held, and Heyoka was helpless, and the bear was coming out of the pines.

Mouse tried to cry out to distract his attention from the colt. Only a gurgle came through the knotted cloth of the gag

Patch Eye had stuffed in his mouth. He began to choke, making a strangling sound. Over by Heyoka the great black form stood up upon its hind legs. It waited motionlessly, the huge forepaw drawn back for the blow that would break the colt's thin neck. Then it dropped back to all fours, circled away from the young horse, disappeared again.

The boy held his breath, the choking controlled. Where was the bear?

Woof! growled Mato, as if in reply to the thought. The breath of the bear was so close to the boy that he could feel it warm and rank upon his face. Mouse turned his head slowly toward the direction of the breathing, then held absolutely still. Above him loomed Mato Sapa.

The bear was looking down at the boy in that curious way he had looked down upon him in the cañon where he had killed old Rainbow. From his chest, when Mouse's eyes met his, rumbled the same muttering growl that had rumbled from it the other time. He put his blunt nose down against the boy's small body. He shoved the nose hard into the boy and took a great whiff of his scent. Then he moved the nose to the face. Mouse could feel the rough, moist nostrils sponging over his neck and ears. The bear exhaled the human odors with a snort, spraying Mouse with dampness. But then he ran his tongue out and licked the lad across the forehead and *woofed* once more. The bear was talking to him precisely as he had when he let Heyoka and himself go free the time before.

Before he could dwell on that happy prospect, however, the bear had forced his muzzle under the boy's back and was trying to turn him over. When he could not do this because of the ropes holding Mouse to the four stakes, he sat down on his haunches, put his forepaws across his paunch, and frowned down at the boy exactly as though he were trying to figure out why he could not turn over an Indian youth who weighed no more than a bee's nest, or a flake of bark.

Presently he put one of the great paws beneath Mouse and tried prying him up as he might a log in search of juicy bugs. Then he noticed one of the ropes. Carefully he put his claws under that rope. Using them as a human would use his fingers, he unearthed the stake to which the rope led as easily as Mouse might pluck a straw from a buffalo chip.

After that, it was but the work of a moment for him to find the other stakes and pull them out of the ground. When he had done that and when Mouse had crawled shakily to his feet, the great bear uttered his grunting *woof* and once more turned and disappeared. For an instant the boy believed that Wakan Tanka had sent the miracle for which he had prayed since kissing the grandmother good bye in her sleep. But the hope was a forlorn one. When Mato turned away from the boy, it was only to return to the colt. He was a bear, after all; he was hungry, and the colt did not carry the same protective scent of memory as did the boy.

Mouse staggered toward the colt, his hands tearing to remove the gag from his mouth. When he had freed his tongue, he cried out to Mato that he must wait, that if he were Mouse's true friend he could not harm the colt. Hearing the shouts, Mato hesitated. The boy was able to reach Heyoka and begin unbuckling his halter to free him before the bear recovered. But Mato would not stop. The hot scent of the young horse was in his nostrils. He did not seem to realize that the boy now stood before him and the colt. Or if he realized it, the killing instinct was too strong for further restraint. The great black paw drew back, the giant form reared upward, the blow was launched at Heyoka's neck.

The colt with a last lunge got his head out of the halter. Away he went, safe and free. But his master was less fortunate. The paw of Mato struck Mouse a glancing blow, only the least fraction of the bear's full power, and only then across the boy's back. Yet so tremendous was the strength in that thick-furred forearm that its mere brush sent the Oglala youth flying like a chip of kindling wood from the blade of a splitting axe.

In the same instant, from the far side of the meadow, a streak of orange flame burst from the pine trees. Mouse heard the heavy bullet whistle over his head, and recognized the sound of the explosion that accompanied it. It was the roar of the Kentucky rifle of Patch Eye Jabez. The white man had stolen back in the night to be certain he killed the great bear by fair means or foul. He had not trusted to the baiting with the young colt or even to the giant bear trap. Wicked and cruel to the end, Patch Eye had returned to murder Mato.

As this thought flashed through Mouse's mind, the boy heard the rifle's bullet strike home into the bear's flesh. He heard, too, the deep grunt of pain with which Mato received the smash of the lead. Peering hard, he saw to his horror that the great bear was down. Yet, even as he watched, Mato surged to his feet again and reared up looking for his enemy.

But Patch Eye was clever. He did not move from the shelter of his ambush. He made no least noise. And he had been wise enough to place himself downwind of the bear. There was no way in which Mato could locate his attacker. There was no way, even, for the bear to know from whence or why came this terrible power that had hurt him so grievously. He could only think of one thing in his pain and surprise. That was to escape from the meadow. To flee to his high home. To seek his cave far up among the rocks below Wakan Tanka's lodge where the winds blew the snow-smoke all the year, and where no man might follow him, and no other bullet find him.

Mouse saw him start to totter toward his freedom, and a

cold fear leaped up within him: the bear was going in the direction of the buried trap. He was already but a stride or three from the grasp of its hidden jaws.

"Mato!" the boy cried out. "Turn aside! Do not take the trail!"

But the bear no longer heeded him. Only pain and confusion guided his path.

Mouse heard the ringing snap of the trap's steel teeth. He heard them grind together in Mato's leg. He heard the brief rattle of the trap's chain, the bumping of the heavy log to which the chain was locked. Then he heard but one other sound up there in the blackness of Mato's road. It was the great bear crying softly to himself from the deepness and the sickness of his wounds.

Chapter Twenty-Three

Patch Eye ran across the meadow toward the trapped bear. He passed so closely by Mouse that the boy could hear his panting curses of triumph. But if the white man had heard the Oglala youth cry out his warning to the bear, or if he now saw him crouched in the grass, he gave no sign.

Up the trail he raced toward the burying place of the trap. Forgetting his own danger, Mouse stole after him. He was in time to see the bear make a final lunge to free himself as his enemy rushed up. His effort broke loose the anchor log of the trap that had become lodged between two boulders. Mouse held his breath, praying that Mato would now fall upon the white man and destroy him. But the bear was too severely injured. His only instinct remained to escape. Painfully the great beast dragged himself up the trail. Behind him the trap, with its chain and anchor log, banged and bumped among the rocks.

Yet Patch Eye did not pursue the telltale sounds. In such darkness and going upward along a steep and narrow mountain track unknown to him beyond this point, the hunter did not dare follow his victim. The best he could manage was to stand and call out after him. "Run hard, Mato!" he shouted wildly. "Run fast! Bleed yourself, waste your strength. Fight the log. Bite the chain. Don't worry about a thing. I will be up to see you with the first daylight! I have a message for you from the Oglala band of Iron Road. It's written on a fine white spirit lance. You will understand it, never fear. Hee hee!"

His quavering laugh died away. There was no answer from Mato. Far above, Mouse could still hear the faint sounds of the trap being dragged behind the bear. As well, he heard the whimperings of pain when the trap twisted itself upon the tortured leg of the desperate animal. Then, while he continued to listen, he heard the sliding of small rocks in the trail near his hiding place. Patch Eye was returning to the meadow.

At once Mouse realized he had stayed too long. Creeping softly away from the trail, he leaped to his feet and ran in a crouch across the meadow. Ahead of him he could see the break in the pine trees where the trail from the granite ledge came down to the meadow. Reaching the foot of the ledge in safety, he clambered up its steep way and hid himself among the boulders at its top. There he lay quietly, straining to catch any sounds of pursuit from below.

None came to him, however. Evidently Patch Eye had *not* heard his warning cry to the bear. If he had seen Mouse struck down by Mato, or if he had witnessed the freeing of Heyoka, he now paid neither event the least attention. He did not even look in the meadow grass to determine if the boy or his colt might be lying there dead or wounded. He simply did not care about them any longer. He had gotten the bear. That was all he cared about. And why not? He had nothing to fear from the Oglala youth and the many-colored colt. The worst they might do was to find the old grandmother and carry a bad tale about Patch Eye down the mountain to Iron Road. But what harm could such a tale do when Patch Eye returned with his proof—the right forepaw of the bear—that he had killed the evil Mato Sapa? Yes, and doing so that he had freed the people of Iron Road from the bear's spirit forever? Ah, no harm at all, indeed, nothing but grateful praise would come to the white man when he had done that. The only thing about which Patch Eye had yet to worry was finishing off Mato with the spirit lance in the morning, and clearly he was not worrying over that matter.

While Mouse shivered upon the ledge, the white man took shelter among the pines. There he built a crackling fire and boiled himself a pot of coffee. The entire time he hummed and whistled eerily to himself, or chuckled and laughed as he talked aloud to his bony old horse. His demented behavior only increased Mouse's chills.

Turning his eyes upward toward the great snows upon Sotoju, the Indian boy prayed to Wakan Tanka to send him some message by which he might aid black Mato in his sad despair, to suggest to his red child, Tonkalla, some weapon with which to destroy the evil white man before the latter might finish off the noble bear. As he raised his plea, there appeared in Mouse's mind a vision as bright as though lit with full sunlight. He saw Patch Eye's old camp where he had aimed Old Caniyassa at the white man in vain. He saw, among the rocks of that camp, something he had surrendered there to Patch Eye—his short Sioux hunting bow and quiver of broad-head arrows—and he saw again the contemptuous way in which the white man had laughed at the crude bow and crooked arrows, and how he had flung them away among the rocks. But Mouse knew more of that little bow and its stubby arrows than did his tormentor. At close range those heavy-headed shafts could cause a crippling wound in any creature that walked on two or four feet and was mortal. The boy got to his feet and thanked Wakan Tanka for answering his prayer. He then set out along the mountainside.

The way was dark and perilous. Low clouds hid the stars. The wind was crying in a lonesome mournful manner that warned Mouse the weather was changing once more, perhaps for the final time. The snow smelled very near. *Hopo, hookahey!* The boy must travel with all haste.

Again Wakan Tanka seemed to guide his red child with belated care, bringing him safely through the gathering storm to the place of the old camp. Nor was that all He brought the boy to. It was when Mouse recognized the rocks ahead of him and quickened his steps to reach them that he saw the flickering glow of the campfire. The blaze was so small, so cleverly hidden by screening boulders, that one could not detect it until almost upon it. The boy knew at once that it must be an Indian fire, but he could not imagine what Indian might possibly have built it there. The question was answered for him by the most welcome sound he had heard in his brief life. It was the old grandmother singing softly to herself a prayer song for her grandson's safety!

Chapter Twenty-Four

Mouse could not restrain his happiness. He uttered a loud cry of greeting as he ran toward the grandmother's fire. The cry startled the old lady. Instead of embracing her grandson, she ran over toward Sunsunla, whom Mouse now noticed for the first time. Seizing the mule's muzzle, she held it shut and prevented him braying a noisy welcome to the returned youth.

"Fool boy!" She glared at Mouse. "Must you run up on me yelling in the night, and getting the mule to bray, so that Patch Eye and everyone else on the mountain will know we are here? Will you never learn to be a good Oglala? *Ih!* What a grandson!"

But all the while she was scolding the lad, she was shedding tears of joy to see him again, fool or no fool.

"Ah—" she grinned—"you will never make a warrior, but what does it matter? We are together once more. All is well."

"Grandmother," Mouse answered, shaking his head, "all is not well. A good friend of ours is in trouble. Patch Eye has captured Mato in a steel trap, and has also shot him with his Kentucky rifle. What can we do?"

"Do you mean what can we do to help the bear?"

"Yes."

"Did the shot kill him?"

"No, no, only a painful wound."

"But he is secure in the trap's jaws?"

"Yes, by one of his legs, I think."

Now it was the grandmother who shook her head. "Then what can we do to help him?" she asked. "What can a small boy, an old lady, and a mule do against that white devil with his Kentucky rifle?"

"I don't know, Grandmother. But I came back to this camp to find my bow and arrows that Patch Eye took from me and threw away here. I thought to try to return and put an arrow into Patch Eye's back, before he could put the spirit lance into Mato's heart tomorrow morning."

"Very brave," said the grandmother. "And very stupid." She patted the boy on the head, seeing that she had injured his pride. "Don't take it so hard about your little bow," she said. "Don't even bother to look for it. I have brought along some special medicine that is much stronger. You will see when the time comes."

"I would rather see right now," insisted the boy. "If you have any special medicine to use against Patch Eye, Grandmother, you had better bring it forth."

"Why, there it is, right over there." The old lady smiled. "It's inside that roll of skins tied to Sunsunla's saddle."

"Not the telescope!" cried Mouse in disappointment.

"The telescope?" frowned the grandmother. "What would I do to Patch Eye with that? Do you think I am crazy?"

"Yes." The boy grinned. "Don't you think so, too?"

"I do," said the old lady, laughing. "Hoo hoo hoo!"

Mouse joined her in the laugh. When they had enjoyed its good feeling, the wrinkled squaw busied herself preparing food. Mouse was nearly starved and ate like a wolf. As he gorged himself, the grandmother told him her story.

It was a simple tale of how Sunsunla had showed up at the house of logs and then guided the old lady back to this abandoned camp of Patch Eye's, needing no tracks to lead him but only depending on his instinct and that wonderful homing quality that all mules have. Before leaving the log house, the grandmother said she had released the other ponies from the pen and driven them toward the outer valley and the exit trail. They would smell the big snow coming, she assured Mouse, and would be wise enough to go out through the crevice in the cliff and back down the mountain, even if she and Mouse did not join them.

When she paused, Mouse recounted his adventures with Patch Eye, concluding with Mato's being shot and trapped, and of his struggle up the mountain toward freedom. When he had finished, the old lady frowned sadly.

"Poor little Clown," she said. "Of course, I sorrow also for the bear, but to lose your young horse, not to know if he is dead or alive. *Ai!* What a pity."

Mouse nodded, overcome at the memory. "Grandmother," he said, "don't you think we ought to pray for the colt? He may still be living."

"Yes," said the old lady, bowing her head. "You go ahead and pray, boy. I will join you."

Mouse also bowed his head, but before he could start the prayer, it was answered. A sound of clopping hoofs came out of the darkness, followed by a long-legged, wobbly-kneed creature with a travel-stained coat of many colors.

"Heyoka!" Mouse cried. "Wakan Tanka be praised, it's you!"

The colt trotted to the fire. He lay down in the sooty dust by its side and rolled. He jumped to his feet, shook out the ashes and dust and soot all over Mouse and the grandmother, kicked up his heels, nipped at Sunsunla, whinnied loudly, and dashed off down to a strip of grass by a nearby mountain spring. There he fell to grazing as calmly as though they had all never been separated, stolen, taken captive, or anything else out of the ordinary.

"Yes, that's Heyoka, all right!" snapped the grandmother. "No other colt could make such a fool of himself. One almost wishes Mato had not missed him with the paw."

"Grandmother," asked Mouse, sobering at the mention of the bear, "what *are* we going to do about Mato?"

The ancient squaw fastened her bright eyes upon the boy. She tapped him with her bony forefinger, speaking with an unusual earnestness. "Mouse, don't think of the bear, think of us. We now have your young horse back. Neither he nor yourself is harmed. I am well. The mule is sound of limb. We can go now. If we leave at once, we can beat Patch Eye to the split cliff trail and be first before him down the lowland trail. I urge you to think hard of this, boy. It is serious."

Mouse knew it was serious. He nodded his dark head but did not reply. The remembering lines grew deeper about his eyes and mouth. He looked far off toward Sotoju. He thought of the blizzard coming so soon on the icy wind. He thought of seeing their people again. He thought of the warm lodges, the hot, roasted meats, the good friends, and the feeling of the heart to be home again. But then he thought of another one: a lonely, injured, and friendless one, one who had no people to flee to, one who lay wounded in the cold and the darkness of the mountainside waiting only for the morning and for death.

"We cannot do it, Grandmother," he said quietly. "Our friend lies bleeding and alone upon the mountain. When the new day comes, we must be at his side to do what we can for him. We cannot leave Mato like that. We are Oglalas."

The old lady sniffed loudly and wiped her eyes. She stamped her foot and cursed the cold wind which, she explained, always made her eyes water in such a fashion. Then she sighed happily.

"I always said you were a fool, Mouse," she told him. "But if you say we stay with the bear, then we stay with the bear.

However," she added sharply, "I believe we had better do some pretty hard praying before we set out to find him. That bear isn't the only one that is going to need some help up on that mountainside. Bow your head."

Mouse obeyed, and the old lady threw a pinch of powdered eagle bone upon the fire. She watched its smoke ascend into the stormy night, then shook her gnarled fist upward.

"You, up there, old Wakan Tanka!" she shouted with a scowl, "I've been praying a long time to you, seventy summers nearly, and I am not too pleased with the answers you have sent me. Do you hear that?" She did not wait for Wakan Tanka to acknowledge the challenge but swept on threateningly. "Now uncover your ears up there and pay attention to what I say this time. Here comes my prayer . . .

> *Tunka sila le iyahpe ya yo,*
> **O Great Father receive these**
> **Humble words of praise and**
> **Gratitude for all the many**
> **Wonderful replies which in**
> **Your generous wisdom you**
> **Have sent this faithful one**
> **In times before this night.**

Mouse, worried by the old squaw's rough tone with the Great Father, stole a glance upward to the wind-whipped snows of Sotoju. He half expected a flash of lightning or a clap of angry thunder to come crashing down upon them in punishment. Yet nothing whatever happened, and the boy shook his head in proud wonderment. His grandmother was a most remarkable woman. Even Wakan Tanka was afraid of her.

Chapter Twenty-Five

They slept a few uneasy hours and were awake long before daylight. They had far to travel, and upon such a trail the darkness was their best companion. The snow had moved nearer. The wind bent the tall pines. When it did so, Mouse could feel the spitting of icy sleet. He and the grandmother looked at one another, knowing their time had shortened during the night. They worked more swiftly.

The mule and the colt had to be left at the camp. Tethering them beneath the shelter of an overhanging rock, the boy tried to be reassuring. "We are not abandoning you," he promised. "We will come back for you. Be easy in your hearts."

The grandmother had more detailed instructions. "Never mind your hearts," she told the animals. "It's your mouths I'm worried about. You, Donkey," she snapped at Sunsunla. "One bray out of you while we are away, and we won't come back for you. We will leave you here for the wolves."

Sunsunla flicked his ragged ears in surrender. Heyoka whickered the soft mustang sound of trust in his master's words. Mouse hugged the colt, then turned away quickly. It was not a happy farewell—who could say if any of them would meet again?

They set out along the trail to the bear trap meadow. Bending into the drive of the sleet, they wrapped their thin blankets hard about them. Their teeth chattered nonetheless, for the icy wind was ever more fierce.

"*Ai-eee!*" cried the grandmother. "Look above you, Mouse. The clouds have come down to the tree tops. *Hopo, hookahey!*"

The boy nodded. He tightened his grip on the hunting bow that he had brought along despite the old lady's advice that he would not need it. Over eastward the light was growing. Soon the day would be upon them. Glancing at the roll of skins which the grandmother had taken from Sunsunla's saddle and slung across her own back, the youth made a silent prayer: the special medicine of Ousta, the Limper, had better prove as strong as she had said it would be!

They came at last to the granite ledge above the meadow. The daylight was still murky, still uncertain. They could see Patch Eye's fire, however, where it lay under the dark pines. A thin streamer of smoke was wisping from it. The smoke curled close to the ground, not rising much.

"He has banked his coals," said the grandmother. "He means to come back to that fire."

"But he's gone!" said Mouse.

"Come on," the old lady said. "We can still catch up with him. He can't have departed very long ago. He would not go up that trail before good daylight."

"Perhaps you are right," agreed the boy. "Not knowing where Mato might be waiting for him, he would not dare to go up there in the dark. We must hurry, though."

They went down the ledge and across the meadow. Panting up the mountain trail beyond, they came to the burial place of the trap.

"Much blood here," said the grandmother. "*Hopo!*"

They toiled upward, knowing they were late in the race to aid the bear. But suddenly they heard ahead of them the voice of Patch Eye, calling out to the wounded animal, and knew then that there might yet be time. And there was.

They came to a low place in the trail. Below them, in this low place, the trail widened to a level rocky space no larger than the pitching ground of two or three teepees. Beyond the level, the trail twisted up into a sheer precipice. At the top of this cliff it seemed to vanish into the cold gray air. The boy and the grandmother knew they were very near Mato's home.

Yet, looking below, they saw that the poor beast was far, far from that home. Indeed, he might never see it again. Through his weakness caused by loss of blood, Mato had fallen into a hole filled with sharp rocks. In his struggles to come out of this place, he had lodged the trap log between rocks and could not move it. Moreover, he had then threshed about and entangled his legs in the trap's chain so that he lay helpless as a newborn cub, able only to turn his head. It was over this pitifully fallen giant of Sotoju that Patch Eye now stood with the spirit lance upraised.

"Quick," Mouse whispered to the grandmother. "He is going to kill Mato. Use your special medicine."

"Yes, yes," answered the old lady, unslinging the roll of skins from her back. "But it is you who must use the medicine, Mouse. Here it is. Take it and put its spell upon Patch Eye Jabez!"

With the words she unfurled the skins and thrust her special medicine into the boy's hands. Mouse's heart leaped, then fell like a stone. What the grandmother had given him was Old Caniyassa, the unfaithful pony herd musket that failed more than it fired. The boy accepted the weapon unhappily.

"Grandmother!" he muttered, "suppose this is the time it chooses not to go off when I press the trigger?"

But the grandmother was of sterner spirit. Before Mouse

could prevent her, she had pushed him out into the open behind Patch Eye and the bear. In the same moment she shouted in Sioux at the bearded hunter.

"Turn around, you sneaking white cur!" she screeched delightedly. "Your time of departing has crept up on you!"

Patch Eye whirled about. He did not see the grandmother who was still wisely staying behind her hiding rock. All that he saw was Mouse, pointing the old musket at his stomach. The Oglala boy was very frightened, but he was not alone. The pink color faded out of Patch Eye's face. He turned as gray as spoiled buffalo fat. When the boy saw that, he knew the white man was also very afraid of him—and he felt a power rise up within him like no power he had ever imagined.

"Grandmother!" he cried, "your special medicine is working. I feel its magic. Come out and take Patch Eye's rifle."

"Boy," croaked the white man, "wait a bit. We can make a bargain here. We are both after the same thing, this black devil of a grizzly bear, are we not?"

"If you move your feet one inch," said Mouse, "I will press this trigger. Stand still!"

Patch Eye stared at him, his single eye burning like a hot coal in the darkness of the coming storm. "Indian boy," he sneered, "I don't believe you've got the courage to press that trigger."

"Patch Eye," said Mouse, returning the stare, "there is one certain way for you to find out. Just move your feet that one inch more."

The white man looked longingly toward his Kentucky rifle where it rested upon the snow. He had left it there to go in and finish Mato with the spirit lance. It would take but a single step for him to reach it. But in the silence of his hesitation, he heard Mouse cock the big hammer of the pony herd musket.

"All right, all right!" he agreed hurriedly. "What is it that you wish me to do?"

Mouse frowned. He glanced back over his shoulder. "Grandmother," he appealed, "what is it that we wish Patch Eye to do?"

Now the old lady came out from behind her rock. She grinned and waved pleasantly at the white man. "*Kola tahunsa,* hello, dear friend and cousin," she greeted him. "What a fine surprise to see you again. How have you been this autumn? We have worried over you."

Patch Eye glared at her suspiciously. He was crazy but not *that* crazy. "Granny," he said, "tell this wild boy to put down the musket so that we may discuss this thing like old friends."

"No," said the ancient squaw, "I have a better idea. You put down the spirit lance. Lay it carefully among the rocks. Otherwise the wild boy will press the trigger."

"Of course." Patch Eye smiled. "That is no problem, granny." He put the lance on a rock, but he was nervous about it, and the weapon fell off and lodged, point upward, among some lower rocks.

"Let it alone!" ordered the grandmother as he started to retrieve the shaft. She turned to Mouse. "Keep the musket watching him," she said. "I will go and bring the ropes and tie him up."

"Good." Mouse nodded. "We can put him across his bony horse and take him down the mountain with us. Iron Road can give him the Oglala trial."

"Exactly what I had in mind," said the old lady. "But watch him now. I would rather trust a skunk with fresh bird eggs than turn my back on a white man."

She brought the ropes and moved to go behind Patch Eye to bind his arms. As she did so, he struck at her like a coiled snake, seizing her and twisting her old body in front of his as a shield.

"Now, then, brave Oglala boy!" He sneered at Mouse. "Let me see you press that trigger when I start to pick up my own rifle *this* time."

"Grandmother . . . !" Mouse started to cry out. But the old lady cut him off with an angry wave. "Stop blubbering and shoot him, boy!" The old squaw's eyes flashed fearlessly. "My few bones won't stop much of that scrap iron you have loaded into Old Caniyassa. Patch Eye will receive his full share of it. Go ahead, shoot!"

But the boy would not do it, of course. Patch Eye Jabez had known that he could not. Grinning his wolf grin, the bearded hunter edged sideways toward his Kentucky rifle.

Chapter Twenty-Six

When Patch Eye had picked up his rifle, he put its muzzle against the grandmother's back.

"Put your old musket on the ground!" he snarled at Mouse.

The boy did so. The moment he had, Patch Eye gave the grandmother a vicious shove, throwing her to the ground. She fell hard and lay very still. The white man did not look at her crumpled form but stepped over it, his single eye fastened upon Mouse.

There was no sound, then, save the labored breathing of Mato in his chains. Even the wind fell still. Patch Eye swung the muzzle of his rifle toward Mouse.

The Indian boy knew the white man was going to shoot him. It was the way in which his lone eye glazed and the way in which his thick lips lifted themselves from the yellow teeth in that expression of evil that Patch Eye thought to be a smile. Beyond all, it was the way in which the bearded hunter's broken-minded laugh startled the silence of the mountainside just before his finger closed upon the trigger of the Kentucky rifle.

"*Hee hee hee hee . . . !*"

It was the last laugh the Oglala boy ever heard from Patch Eye Jabez. As the white man uttered it, the grandmother rose on her hands and knees behind him. She seized his leg with the grasp of a striking hawk and she buried her three snag-like teeth to the gum line in the calf of that leg.

Patch Eye shrieked with rageful pain. He tried to twist about and smash at the old squaw with the butt of his rifle, but he was too late. The grandmother threw a loop of the tying rope about his feet and tripped him. Patch Eye went sprawling. He fell heavily on his back among the trailside rocks. Strangely he did not move after he fell. Believing he had struck his head and was unconscious, Mouse ran toward the grandmother to get the rope and tie him up before he might regain his senses.

But the old lady withheld the rope from him. "You will not need this," she said. "Wakan Tanka has bound his limbs forever."

Halted by the dark tone of her words, Mouse looked more closely at the place where Patch Eye lay among the rocks. His face paled, and he felt unwell. The white man had fallen precisely where the spirit lance of the Oglala people had laid wedged point upward. The long steel blade of the weapon had driven through his heart, pinning him to the frozen earth.

The old grandmother nodded at the boy and looked upward through the swirling snowflakes now beginning to descend. Her eyes were upon the summit of holy Sotoju, the eternal teepee of the Great Spirit.

"*Ha-ho,* thank you, Wakan Tanka," she murmured.

Mouse's face was still as pale as that of the dead white man. But the grandmother was not one to waste time over such small matters.

"Come on, boy," she said. "Feel the ice in the spittle of that wind! Feel the sting of those fat snowflakes! We must hurry."

They set to work about the dangerous business of freeing Mato. The great bear watched them, not moving, not making a sound. They did not know what he might be thinking, what

197

he might do to injure them, when they had released him from the trap and chain. Whatever it was, they must risk it, for among the Oglalas a life is always offered for a life—and the great bear had spared them both in his time.

"First," directed the grandmother, "we must take the tangled chains from his legs. In that way the trap will still hold him should he try to harm us."

It was a supreme test of courage, unwinding the chain from the enormous limbs of Mato Sapa, but the bear lay as patiently as some huge black dog, his eyes following them as they toiled over him, watching them, watching, watching.

At last the chain was free; only the trap remained. But the only way in which they could force apart the jaws of the trap was to find a pole long enough to pry them open, and the only pole on that bare mountainside was a lone pine limb jammed into a rock slide above them. The slide was as high as four teepees, holding a thousand times a thousand tons of loose rock and huge boulders. If they pulled the pine limb loose, it might release the entire mountainside above them, burying them alive *with* the bear.

The grandmother stared up at the slide. She nodded spryly. She threw aside her tattered blanket, spat upon her wrinkled hands.

"Nevertheless, Mouse," she said to the boy, "we must pluck out that pine limb from the mountain."

So it began.

A dozen times the rocks above them started to move, but finally they had worked the pine limb free and could use it to pry open the trap. Gradually, gradually, the rusted jaws were forced apart and away from the wounded leg of Mato Sapa. At last the trap was pried completely open.

"Mato," said the grandmother, "do exactly what I say and no more. Do you understand?"

The great bear made a soft *woof* in his throat.

"All right," said the old lady. "Now draw out your leg. Slowly, slowly. Do not touch the trap's jaws with it. If you do, the trap may spring away from us and close on you again. It might break the bone. Then nothing could help you. *Waste*, pay attention now. Bring out the leg.

The bear understood. With a care and intelligence nearly human, he eased the leg from between the gaping trap jaws. Only in the last instant did he make a small error, allowing his claws to touch the trap's jaws. The slight jarring was enough. The pine limb slipped. The trap's jaws smashed together with a ringing clang.

Still they were too late. Mato Sapa was free. The only part of him which he left behind in the steel teeth of the trap were the middle two claws of his right forefoot, together with a shred of his gleaming black fur. These were the mementos that Mouse and the grandmother bore away from that lonely place to remember Mato by. What the bear bore away with him to keep the Indians in his savage memory, the boy and the old lady could not say. But Mouse was certain that he took something with him. In truth, the Oglala boy knew that he did. Mato took their hearts with him.

The last they saw of the great bear was as he paused at the top of the cliff trail. They had watched him make his way slowly up the steep path toward his unknown home. By the way that he went, growing in strength with each step, they knew that he would survive. The bullet of Patch Eye had broken no bones, severed no main artery. Neither had the trap done irreparable harm. A good winter's sleep in his warm cave and Mato Sapa would come down again with the spring songbirds and the new grass into his beautiful Valley of the Sunflowers.

But up there on the cliff trail now he was saying good bye

to his Indian friends. The grandmother raised her arm in the farewell sign. She waved to Mato, saluting him.

"*Wagh!* old bear . . . sleep well!" she called.

Mouse, unashamed of the tears that filled his eyes, also waved and called aloud. "*Woyuonihan,* Mato! I salute you. Keep me always in your heart, as I keep you!"

For a moment the returning blizzard held its breath. In the fleeting stillness the old squaw and her grandson thought they heard Mato send down to them the soft deep *woof* they knew so well. They always believed that he had heard their farewells and replied to them. Yet before they could make certain of this, the snows whipped in about them, blotting out the cliff trail. They strained their eyes to catch and their ears to hear some final sign from Mato Sapa, but there was only the howl of the blizzard wind and the white silent wall of the snow. They never saw the great black bear again.

Chapter Twenty-Seven

There remained some final happenings concerning Mouse and the grandmother that should be told in justice to the old lady. When they turned away from peering upward toward the vanished Mato, making ready to go away from that place as quickly as they might, the grandmother glanced about frowningly.

"Wait a moment, Mouse," she said. "Where is that cursed pony herd rifle of yours?"

The boy found the weapon and gave it to her.

"Thank you." She nodded. "I only wanted to see what magic would have happened with my special medicine if you had only pressed the trigger." She raised the rifle and fired it with the usual result. The hammer fell with a dull clink, and the gunpowder did not ignite.

"Ah, ha! just as I thought." The old lady threw the rifle from her. It landed among the rocks down in the hole where Mato had been imprisoned by the trap. "Useless thing, stay there and rot!" she shouted. "Your medicine is weaker than stale tea water!"

But the grandmother was wrong. The pony herd rifle had not lost its special medicine. When it fell into the hole, it exploded with a roar that shook the mountain. There was a frightening pause, then the great slide of rocks above the hole commenced to move.

"Look out!" yelled Mouse. "Run for your life!"

The old lady did not need the advice. She passed Mouse as though the boy were standing in deep mud. A moment later both of them were safely behind the nearby turning of the trail. There they crouched, watching the great slide thunder down and cover for all time the trail to Mato Sapa's high home and to cover, also, the evil form of Patch Eye Jabez and the finally honored frame of Old Caniyassa.

"Well," chirped the grandmother, when the last rock had fallen, "that wasn't such a bad trade, eh? What do you think, boy?"

It was then that Mouse saw she had somehow managed to rescue Patch Eye's beautiful Kentucky rifle on the run. She held the priceless weapon out toward her grandson now, her three-toothed grin spreading to both ear-lobes.

"Here," she said. "A good warrior needs a good rifle."

Mouse accepted the rifle, saying nothing. But then of what use were words? When a woman has called a boy a warrior, she can say no more, nor can he answer anything to her.

They set off down the mountain at a brisk trot. Reaching the bear trap meadow, they sought out Patch Eye's pony gelding and mounted on him. The old animal was glad to see them and carried them with willing eagerness back to the old camp. There, they freed Sunsunla and Heyoka. The grandmother rode the mule while Mouse stayed with the old gelding. Behind them came Heyoka, whinnying and kicking up his heels at the falling snow.

At the mouth of the exit trail through the cliff they found their other ponies waiting for them, rumps turned to the freezing wind. The grandmother whacked them all good with her driving stick, and led the way through the darkness of the narrow chasm. Mouse looked back for a last sight of Sunflower Valley, Mato's home, the lonely and mysterious lost high valley of the great bear. But he could no longer see through the snow, and the scream of the blizzard wind was like a wild beast in its fury. It was a good thing to be in the warm darkness of the cliff's heart and to hear ahead the gay, cracked singing voice of his old grandmother and by his side the soft mustang whickering of his many-colored colt.

The boy turned his eyes upward in the darkness and had some private things to say to Wakan Tanka. A few minutes after that they reached the daylight of the other side.

Chapter Twenty-Eight

When they came through the great cliff and out upon the other side of the mountain, the sun was shining brilliantly. It was that autumn softness of a day that the Oglalas called the Indian Summer. Mouse would not have believed that such beauty could exist so near to the blizzard's cold. Yet there was even more than the day's warmth to greet them as they emerged from Mato's land.

Taking out the brass telescope, the grandmother passed the instrument to Mouse. "Look down there along the road to the lower country," she told the boy. "Fix the glass upon that place where I sat on the rock when we decided to take Mato's road. Tell me what you see passing by our rock."

Mouse focused the telescope, wondering what put the excitement in her words. Then his own eyes widened.

"It's our village!" he cried. "The People are moving down to the low country for the winter. I see old Turtle, and Fox, and there is Bald Head. Ah, what a wonderful thing to see them all again!" He lowered the telescope, face grown darkly sorrowful. "But would it not be a far more wonderful thing," he said, sighing, "if we might only go with them as in the old days?"

The grandmother cocked her head to one side. "What is that you say?" she inquired with her bird-like pertness. "Do you mean to tell me that you don't think the People will welcome us back? Are you saying they will refuse to permit us to rejoin the band? Well, cheer up, boy!"

"How can I cheer up?" inquired Mouse glumly. "When Mato was not killed with the spirit lance through his heart, we lost our only chance of returning to the band. You know that. Yet you tell me to cheer up?"

Now the grandmother gave the saddened youth her very sharpest look. "Fool boy," she said. "Don't you understand that when Patch Eye fell on the spirit lance and it pierced his heart, Wakan Tanka was putting the white man in the bear's place? Wakan Tanka was trading us Patch Eye's life for Mato's life, and Patch Eye's spirit for Mato's spirit. So when we got rid of the white man's evil spirit, we were getting rid of the black bear's evil spirit. What could be more clear? It's all very simple when you understand it."

Mouse stared at her, shaking his head in bewilderment. But he was getting back his old grin, nevertheless. It was not possible to stay downcast or to be defeated around old Ousta, the Limper.

"Grandmother," he said, "you will never bring it to pass, but I salute you anyway. You have the spirit of a dozen bears and a hundred white men. *Wagh!*"

"What?" she shouted indignantly. "You dare to doubt my ability to tell my tale to Iron Road and the other old addle-pates on the council of elders? Hah!"

Mouse touched his forehead in the respect sign.

"I still salute you," he said. "You have the mind of a mad coyote and the merciful instincts of a starving wolf, Grandmother. But you will need more than that to convince Iron Road and those old men that Mato's evil spirit has been driven from us."

"Boy," the old squaw cackled, "I have not begun to reveal to you the resources of your grandmother's ability to tell a tale. Listen," she said, her crinkling grin and bright eyes making her ancient face sparkle, "don't you realize that with that small patch of Mato's paw fur and those two long middle claws of his right forefoot which you carry in your belt pouch you will become the greatest Sioux since Chief Stirring Bear? *Ih!* Wait until I get through telling the band about the way you did for Patch Eye with the spirit lance. Wait until I describe for them the manner in which you threw the pony herd rifle at the mountain and brought the vast rock slide thundering down across Mato's road to destroy for all time the mortal trail of the great black spirit bear! Why, boy, when I have finished with you, you will be famous! *Wagh, he-haw!*"

With the words, she leaned over with her driving stick and gave Mouse a cheerful stinging whack.

"*Hookahey!*" she yelled. "Let's go! If we are to sit up here weeping all day on the mountainside, we shall never be in time to join the band for the trip to the low country. Come, Grandson Mouse. Let us gallop down there and greet those lucky people. I can scarcely wait to tell them of their great fortune in having us back again!"

With that she began to laugh. In a moment Mouse joined her. They put their arms about one another and sat there on their mounts, cackling as happily as two loons on a blue lake at sunset. Then they looked at each other and shouted— "*Wagh!*"—*and kicked their riding animals in the ribs and set off down the mountainside at breakneck speed.*

Sunsunla, Heyoka, and the four old pack ponies joined in the race as recklessly as the grandmother and the boy. They did not appear to worry any more than did their Indian masters over the quality of their brain power. Their spirits were all glad together and that was the important thing.

FROM WHERE THE SUN NOW STANDS

Will Henry

Five-time Winner of the Spur Award

Surely one of the most dramatic campaigns of the Indian wars was also one of the last—the Nez Perce campaign. And one of the greatest chiefs was the mighty Chief Joseph. Here, with the understanding and insight that only Will Henry could bring to it, is the Spur Award-winning novel of those 113 days in the summer of 1877 when Chief Joseph reluctantly led his people in a rear-guard action from the Nez Perce reservation in Oregon to Montana, across more than one thousand miles of trackless country. Here is a saga of loyalty and treachery, tragedy and triumph, a masterful achievement from the one and only Will Henry.

___4708-X $4.99 US/$5.99 CAN